THE BALD IDENTITY

Trey Bald

iUniverse, Inc.
New York Bloomington

The Bald Identity

iUniverse books may be ordered through booksellers or by contacting:

iUniverse
1663 Liberty Drive
Bloomington, IN 47403
www.iuniverse.com
1-800-Authors (1-800-288-4677)

ISBN: 978-1-4401-4637-4 (pbk)
ISBN: 978-1-4401-4638-1 (ebook)

Printed in the United States of America

iUniverse rev. date: 5/13/09

Scientific research shows that women see bald men as older. However, there is also ample evidence that any given female set of eyes can interpret baldness as intensely arousing. The problem is, this is on an individual basis, whereas the studies look at societal attitudes. In one a study, researchers made two campaign flyers. One had a picture of a 35-year-old bald man, the other the same man but with hair. A much higher percentage of people favoured the guy with hair. There hasn't been a bald president since Eisenhower. This is changing, mostly because attractive men like Michael Jordan or Bruce Willis are taking back their baldness."

Quote stolen from the Brotherhood of Bald People Website

Who is Trey Bald?

My name is Trey Bald and I have been losing my hair since the age of twenty three.

In this book you will notice that I have occasional contrasting views on male pattern baldness. I would like to stress that I did indeed suffer psychologically as a result of my losing hair, but along the way my incredible journey that has taken me all over the world has left me a better person.

I now possess a far deeper understanding of baldness and what it is, so much so that the state of my own hair is irrelevant in comparison to the information I have collected over the last six years.

I have worked for a classified government special ops team in order to put a stop to terrorism conducted by individuals for reasons that involve men's hair or a lack of hair. I can't be any more specific than that.

If the motivation was hair related, my team was called in. In many cases I have left names out. This is to protect the innocent and to avoid breaking the law. All of my work is highly classified and as a result of this there is a lot of information that I'm unable to share with you.

As well as recounting a few stories from missions that I've undertaken, I have included some more personal information and thoughts. This is because I want you, the reader, to know that as well as being a highly trained agent, I'm still just a human being. Just like you, but a little bit better at most things.

As you read on you will learn about my ever changing life, whether it's a personal relationship or my career, there's rarely a dull moment.

I try to have no personal standpoint or opinion on baldness (but I'm only human, and my emotions can cloud my judgement at times). It is whatever it is to the beholder. Some people feel cursed, whilst others live their lives without missing a step.

I hope that some of my experiences and knowledge will be useful to you, and most importantly, educate you on the depths of male pattern baldness.

The Awakening

As a teenager with hair, before I answered my calling as a defender of the bald, I had a strict routine in place. Hair is there to be toyed with, and never trust anyone who thinks otherwise.

It is the single most important defining feature anyone can have, and I've seen it used to maximum effect in my years working undercover.

Spies have been able to walk straight through a room of enemies undetected simply by changing their parting or adding gel/wax/paste to create an altogether different look. Sportsmen have been able to alter the direction their hair grows in order to obtain maximum benefits from the wind direction, either increasing their speed or controlling it.

One method I employed at school with the sole purpose of attracting the opposite sex was the 'dry by night.' The beauty was in its simplicity.

After a hard day I would take a shower and wash my hair, but instead of drying it, I'd spike it up and head straight to bed. With consistent turning over throughout the night my hair was pressed from either side as it dried creating the ultimate Mohawk the following morning.

It wasn't just any Mohawk, it had real style and calibre to it, confusing my opponents and sending the opposite sex into delirium. The only problem was I'd become a target. Bald people resented me and those with hair felt I was making a mockery of their gift.

As I left a Chinese restaurant on a school night, I was approached by a young and attractive lady who claimed to have lost her wallet. Naturally I wasn't going home without helping her recover the item so I instructed my girlfriend at the time to wait in the car with the engine running and the heater on.

As I followed the damsel in distress round the corner my hair told me that something wasn't quite right, but I put it down to irrational paranoia.

There was no wallet around the corner. Instead I came face to face with fifteen members of the notorious 'Hairs Angels', who are well known for their dedication and belief in keeping hair modest and tidy. I was deemed 'dirty' for my 'dry by night' method, word had clearly spread about town that I was pushing the boundaries with my innovative hair style.

Although I managed to put up a fight I was no match for the men that came at me with everything from scissors to the very latest clippers from Japan. I had to respect the quality of their ambush, they had been trained well.

Paranoia is there for a reason. It's what keeps you safe. Anxiety is what helps you survive. All of these supposed negative emotions are the reason we're the number one race on the planet. I forgot that on this particular night.

During my recovery I slowly began to realise there was more to life than my Mohawk, but I was still searching for answers. I read with some interest about how hair loss can be associated with stress, paranoia and anxiety.

I began to wonder whether it was really my hair telling me something was wrong before I was attacked or whether it was some kind of bald premonition. Was this a sign that my hair was not as thick and funky as I thought? Was my imminent baldness trying to keep me safe?

The Unstoppable Power That Is Hairnergy

Hairnergy is a complicated mix of energy that combines the emotion of anger, often thought to be the rage that a bald man feels at losing his hair, and adrenalin. It is an energy only possessed by those suffering from male pattern baldness and if not controlled can have devastating consequences.

Some cases have shown that the subjects strength and pain threshold can increase by up to one million percent.. Hairnergy is created by consistent thought, usually worrying, over the state and advancement of one's hair loss.

When I was starting to lose my hair I had a conversation with my sister who enthusiastically described a good friend of hers who'd been using the hair loss drug Propecia.

I was immediately interested, more so by the fact that this was a guy my age who had clearly been feeling the same sense of loss as myself but had actually taken the plunge and invested some serious capital into treating it. Apparently he had some serious hair going on, the thickest of the thick, so I was excited to meet him

The following week I e mailed him. I had many questions about the drug and wanted to make sure everything was one hundred percent safe before I committed myself. I was surprised at the speed of response and the sheer detail that every one of his e mails contained. Some were like essays with well over a thousand words. This lad had done his homework.

A few weeks later and we set up a meeting. I entered the café at around eleven a.m. on a Saturday morning. It was December, and the streets were cold and icy.

The meeting point was remote to say the least, I couldn't quite believe I was in London, it was more like Chernobyl. My new friend was already seated towards the back of the café, sipping what looked like a white chocolate mocha, though I couldn't be too sure. With a reassuring smile, he beckoned me over to the table and ordered a peppermint latte, one of my favourite drinks, which arrived within ten seconds.

"So Trey, tell me about your hair loss."

Straight to business. Something was wrong. No one can make a peppermint latte in under ten seconds. How did he know I'd order a peppermint latte?

"How often do you think about your hair?"

Another question. If I didn't know any better I'd have considered him a little desperate for information.

"Drink your latte, it'll get cold."

I stood up.

"Who the hell are you," I whispered, staring at the smiling man in front of me.

"Calm down Trey. It will be a lot easier for you if you just relax."

I never felt the blow to my head. When I came round I was in a large white room full of beeping machinery, with wires strapped on to my head. Lots of wires. A familiar looking man entered the room. It was him. My new friend turned enemy.

"Tell me something Trey, do you often meet up with strangers you e mail?"

Keep him talking I thought. The first trick in the book is to make the enemy feel in control of the situation.

"I don't know what you want from me. But please, let me go, I'm not going to go to the police. I just want to stay alive."

The man looked faintly amused. Approaching the computer in the corner of the room, he sat down and studied the figures flying across the screen. Muttering some kind of curse under his breath he picked up the phone next to the keyboard and relayed his information.

"Quinn, it's me. I'm afraid I'm not getting any results. Wherever he's keeping it, he knows what he's doing."

He hung up the phone and strode towards me with some purpose. The few minutes he'd spent away from me were all that Trey Bald needed to take affirmative action. I'd already managed to free both hands using my hairnergy.

"I don't know how you're doing it Trey, but you are going to tell me exactly where….."

He never had a chance to finish his sentence as I kicked downwards onto the side of his left kneecap. Howling in pain he started to fall to the floor but not before I'd followed up with a swift blow to his solar plexus with the palm of my hand.

I moved quickly to the computer to check on the results. Thankfully, there was no evidence pointing to the location of my hairnergy, but I had an even bigger problem now.

Who was Quinn and why had he hired someone to kidnap me? Was my own sister involved?

Remembering exactly what Jason Bourne did in the first Bourne film, I grabbed a map of the building from the wall and tried to find the best exit. I was already feeling drained from the use of my hairnergy but I ghosted up the flight of stairs and found an exit on the second floor.

The cool London snow broke my fall as I jumped from the window and in seconds I was beyond capture, much to the anger of the four armed men that had been alerted to my escape.

I looked back at them knowing they couldn't take a shot at me. It was broad daylight and if any of the events were to become public then whatever operation they were running would have been seriously compromised.

Once I had reached the safety of the streets I immediately purchased some sugar free gum, but I had too much adrenalin to chew. I needed to calm down. I found the closest Borders book shop which also had a Starbucks and grabbed a vanilla latte before heading to the biography section to read about Al Pacino.

The Girl From Biarritz

After the stress and trauma of the betrayal I needed to get away for a week in the sun. I chose Biarritz after hearing good stories about the surf down there.

When you're overlooking a never ending beach full of Mediterranean beauties and clear sea it's hard to imagine a better life and even harder to imagine what it's going to feel like when you're sitting on a rickety plane heading back to the real world of checking e mails and watching the news.

I didn't have time to prepare myself for the girl who was about to bring me the bill for my coffee but I definitely didn't waste any time in trying out my French and lining up a drink for the following day.

The funny thing about people who consider themselves shy when it comes to asking someone out is that when you see someone that has such a profound affect on you all of those old beliefs fly out the window.

It didn't really matter what was going to happen, all I knew was that I would be taking this girl out before I left in forty eight hours. Wait, forty eight hours. That's not enough time. I was going to need the big guns.

Throwing things left and right I tore into my cupboard with a vengeance and pulled out the deadly blue and white seventies style evening shirt with a prominently large collar. It was an ideal weapon for deflecting away from the thinning hair on top of my dome.

The blue could bring out my eyes, the collar would take care of the hair and the professional fit would ensure I looked ten times more athletic than I actually was.

And so began my first date in Biarritz. I managed to find out the all important details. Her name was Marie. She was twenty years old, aspired to be an actress and had an older and younger sister.

The older sister was currently having trouble coming to terms with the fact that her boyfriend was leaving for Australia and the younger sister was just the younger sister.

We finished up our drinks and went for a long walk around the island taking in some of the breath taking views and conversing in an interesting mix of English, French and Spanish.

There was debate over the acting prowess of Edward Norton plus my usual tale of meeting Mixmaster Mike from the Beastie Boys which I'm not sure she fully understood. I even made it back to her flat to meet the younger sister, but eventually the time had come to head back to my place and let her go to dinner with her older and heartbroken sister.

For one reason or another I lost contact with Marie once I returned to London. Strong evidence points to the fact that I pushed her a little hard by turning up to her café a few times before I left with nothing to say other than show how needy I was.

However, being a true professional I had to know for sure. I had to know that it had nothing to do with her ex-boyfriends incredible hair in comparison with my baby like wisps.

A few months later I was back in Biarritz and across the road from Marie's flat in a white unmarked van.

With me I had the usual supplies: a bionic ear that can hear and record sounds from up to three hundred feet away, x2 GSM bugs that make use of the mobile network, x 5 button sized cameras that I needed to place inside the flat and finally an undetectable USB Keylogger that would pull any data from her home computer.

I put my 'Pierre' name tag on my black overalls that told the unsuspecting eye I was in the building for a routine gas check up and crossed over the street with my bag in hand.

On the fourth day I left the bed and breakfast and went to the back of my rented unmarked white van. It had been a frustrating three days. My equipment in the back had been playing up and I was seriously considering a letter of complaint to the manufacturers. Furthermore I'd had no results.

She hadn't mentioned me once in the last three days and I'd only been gone ten weeks.

Just when I thought it couldn't be any worse I had a life line. My tracking device had intercepted an e mail with the subject "re: English boy".

How had I missed the original e mail? What had I spent all those thousands of pounds on? I could have simply hacked into her computer myself. I read through the e mail. It didn't seem to have much to do with me until I stumbled across a few lines mocking my baldness. She had even said what a shame it was considering how good looking she'd found me but that she would never allow herself to be seen in public with a bald man

I knew it. I hadn't been naïve or paranoid, I was right all along. Heartbroken and tired I switched off the machinery and lay in the back of the van. It had been a long and arduous process, but definitely worth it.

I could return home now, safe in the knowledge that balding and bald men are still in grave danger. Had I not gone to so much trouble, complacency may have slipped in, leading me into a false sense of security and well being.

The following morning I picked the opportune time to break into the apartment and recover the surveillance I'd placed. The van was parked a few streets away and had my ticket, passport and some emergency money.

I worked quickly, this wasn't the first time Trey Bald had been under pressure and it wouldn't be the last. By the time I reached the keyboard for my USB, things looked like they were going to go without a hitch.

That was when I heard the footsteps.

I moved like a ninja as the door opened and found a resting place on one of the high beams below the ceiling.

Who the hell was this and why didn't I know they were coming? It looked like a possible friend who had borrowed a set of keys, but either way they'd picked the wrong place at the wrong time. With all the skill of trained soldier I released my grip and came crashing down on the unidentified intruder.

It was a man, and a strong one, I needed to be quick. Locking him in my sleeper hold I clung on until he slipped from consciousness, before I swiftly moved him over to the sofa. He wouldn't remember a thing. I grabbed the USB and put it in the bag with the rest of my kit and headed for the door, adrenalin pumping.

Back in the van I knew I'd been careless, and it could have cost me.

On arrival at the airport I selected one of my many wigs for the check in and a different passport. Trey Bald would not be flying today.

I was Robin Bogenhart, a Swedish scientist with curly blonde locks, returning from a brief business trip.

Treatments

Whilst on the plane I continued to work on my research regarding hair loss treatments.

- Finasteride
- Dutasteride
- Minoxidil
- Green tea
- Caffeine (a coffee a day keeps the baldness away)
- Hedgehog agonists
- Copper peptides
- Scalp massage

Just one of my many undercover assignments included an eight month period in a small town ten kilometres north of Moscow.

My group and I had gathered strong intelligence suggesting that there was an ongoing scam of unproven treatments for male pattern baldness and the victims were paying an extortionate amount of money to receive them.

One such scam involved a clinic that would hang men upside down two metres above the ground with their head placed in a bucket of worms.

The theory behind this was that by hanging upside down, the blood flow could be redirected to the hair follicles whilst the worms gently massaged the scalp, stimulating the hair which would encourage re-growth.

One victim ended up wasting his life savings on the treatment which, needless to say, did not improve his baldness.

It took me six weeks of continuous intelligence gathering that included bugging the phones, obtaining incriminating photographs and tracking all known assailants until I was able to present a case strong enough for a conviction.

The guilty party were lead by a man named Roman, who was a former psychologist. Using his skills, Roman was able to sense vulnerability and stupidity like a shark senses blood in the water. The people stood no chance.

Its cases like this that make me get up each and every day. I have a duty to protect the innocent and the bald.

In another assignment I found myself spending a considerable amount of time in a Brazilian brothel, where amongst the usual services, men were able to have their head sandpapered, in order to remove the upper layer of skin that was preventing hair from getting through.

Bald men were being convinced that their hair was simply trapped and by taking no action not only were they suffering from baldness but the hair that was trapped was steadily making it's way down and through to the brain with life threatening consequences.

My advice to any aspiring hair person is to take plenty of aerobic exercise and eat lots of wheat based cereals.

The key to hair loss is to lower the levels of DHT (Dihydrotestosterone), an active metabolite of the hormone testosterone and the primary contributing factor to male pattern baldness.

With enough funding, my team and I have been working on a drug aptly named 'Anti DHT' which I'm hoping will soon be available in the form of a chocolate bar.

With the expenses it is likely that these chocolate bars will be fairly pricey at first but the goal is to get even distribution on a global scale at affordable prices. 80% of the proceeds will help fund my future operations in the field of Counter Baldism across the world.

A Danish Princess

For security reasons no names other than my own are mentioned.

This is a story of courage under fire, dealing with pressure and true love. It all happened during one particularly hot summer. Whilst working on a separate mission I received an urgent call from the Danish royal family.

One of their own had gone missing after an evening out with friends in Copenhagen.

Normally I would have sent out a special ops team instead of going it alone but there was another motivating factor. The girl in question was someone from my past.

When I was seventeen years old with the classic bed hair look, I travelled to Denmark to visit the Royal palace on a school trip. Like any teenager all I was interested in was trying to buy cigarettes whilst chasing every girl in the vicinity with my friends.

The last day saw us at the Royal palace not really enjoying a one hour tour full of facts and Danish history.

I snuck off for a quick Marlboro Medium (9 mg Tar, 0.9 mg Nicotine) in the palatial gardens.

Finding a nice patch of sun by the rose bush I inhaled deeply and closed my eyes to the warm rays thinking about how carefree my life was.

When I opened them again I found an altogether different view. Before me stood a young girl about my age, so beautiful that the word beautiful didn't even come close to describing her.

She had brown hair, green eyes and a smile that could break the Devil's heart. Her skin was so perfectly created that I was scared of anything touching it in case it became blemished or smudged. She looked at me and spoke in a cool tone.

"Who are you?"

I inhaled deeply and blew out a fresh plume of smoke.

"I'm Trey Bald."

She stepped forward and put her lips millimetres away from mine. I could feel her sweet breath, and I could only assume that she'd used some form of apricot lip gloss given the arousing scent that made my head spin.

"Nice to meet you Trey Bald."

And with that she turned and walked elegantly into the distance.

Back in the present, I put the phone down and thought the situation over. They had taken my girl. But how did I know the victim in question was the very same girl whose lips I'd nearly touched?

Just recall my story from Biarritz. There is no man more romantic than Trey Bald. I made it my business to find out everything about that girl from the moment she left me.

For years I'd traced e mails, phone calls, received photos. There was not a day that went by that I didn't know what she was doing.

Until now. I'd become so consumed in saving others that I'd forgotten my first love. How could this have happened?

The threat was simple. She had been taken by a group of extremists who threatened to keep her hostage for up to three months without *ever* washing her hair.

I just couldn't stand by and let that happen. Not to that beautiful hair. It deserved to be shampooed and conditioned, curled and straightened, and not with any old product.

With the very best, something like Herbal Essences or Schwarzkopf.

I took the first available flight to Denmark. My team had already managed to trace the incoming terrorist calls and confirmed my location, an abandoned warehouse north of ⊠rhus.

I was going to do this alone.

I saw the first sniper seconds after my first approach. I was only 30 metres away from the building, and he was clearly an amateur, crouching down in the most obvious spot on the roof of an adjacent building.

I spotted some cover ten metres ahead, a large pile of used tyres. Using my newly shaved head I tilted it at a seventy two degree angle deflecting the sun right into my sniper's sights. I could see him flinch in temporary discomfort and it was all the time I needed to get behind the tyres. I knew he'd lost me and he'd be making the call to his superiors. It didn't matter. I had all the time in the world.

Opening my bag I took out the giant can of Wella hairspray and attached my small explosive device. It wasn't much but I didn't exactly have enough time to pick up the heavy artillery.

The extremists had rushed down to the entrance. I counted five of them, not including the sniper who still held his position. If they had been pros I'd already be dead.

Poking my bald head out once more I deflected another beam of sunlight straight into the sniper's eyes. In the spare seconds I had, I launched the Wella hairspray explosive right into the middle of my waiting party at the entrance.

The explosion ripped through the yard as I huddled behind the tyres Rolling out from my cover, I made a run for it, but just yards away from the entrance a bullet clipped my leg causing me to stumble. I pulled myself into the warehouse as the sniper came just inches away from hitting me again, this time the bullet ricocheting of the warehouse doors like an out of control squash ball

I was running out of time, so I grabbed a weapon from the debris and limped as best I could up the stairs. She was in the back room, tied to a chair.

I burst in and moved swiftly to untie her. I could tell that she recognised me.

"Your hair……it's gone?"

"A lot's changed since I was seventeen. But you're still as beautiful as I remember."

"I always knew I'd see you again Trey Bald."

I ushered her to her feet.

"Please, we don't have much time. We need to get out of here."

We moved back through the building towards the stairs and down to the entrance. I had no way of telling where the sniper was or whether he was even in the room preparing an attack. It was my princess who saw him coming though, by the reflection on the back of my bald head. She cried out.

"Trey!"

I spun round as the sniper pounced on me, grabbing my throat trying to close the wind pipe. I struggled to pull the curling irons from my pocket but with my remaining strength I dealt him a blow more severe than he'd ever felt in his short life. We were safe at last.

We spent the night at a cheap hostel, locked in a room until I could arrange safe transportation back to the Royal palace.

It had been two days since she'd washed her hair. Stepping into the shower I found her to be exactly as I'd always imagined, and with a smile she handed me the bottle of Pantene Pro-V

Not the shampoo I'd expected, but this was a moment I was going to enjoy.

The Longing For Belonging

Good Bald

- Decent sized head
- Prominent facial features
- Tan
- Designer stubble (bonus)

Bad Bald

- Peanut head
- Pale complexion
- Doughy face
- No notable features

Above are the general examples of what people consider to be a good bald man or a bad bald man. Naturally it's grossly unjust as many people exercise no control over their own genes and what their natural appearance is.

This has led to a great divide in the bald community, and instead of showing mutual respect and support there have been separate factions forming independently which has led to a very high risk of civil war.

Back in the day, the only tension for bald people came from the well known 'Kill All Bald People' (**K.A.B.P**) faction that formed in the late 80's just outside of San Diego, California. However, there are now independent bald groups that fight their battles not just against groups like the K.A.B.P, but against their own kind.

The most well known rivalry exists between the 'Good looking bald dudes' (**G.L.B.D)** and 'Bald guys that don't look good and don't care' (**B.G.T.D.L.G.A.D.C)**.

Such is the strength of rivalry between these two particular groups that I had to re-think what I believed in. Perhaps people with hair weren't the problem. Perhaps the bald community's biggest problem was with itself. Now that enough people were bald it seemed like human nature to seek out a new reason to join separate sides and wage war with each other.

To make matters worse I learnt of an unprovoked assault on an old friend of mine.

Back when I knew him he was the golden boy of University night life. If you wanted to go somewhere, he was the man to ask.

He ran the door of every fashionable nightclub in the city, and he did it with great humility and style. Everyone knew him, and whether they liked him or not (jealousy is a terrible thing), he was a prominent figure in his endless array of designer clothes

The reason for this senseless attack? His fantastic head of hair.

To this day I've never seen anything like it. It was almost like another living being was perched on his head. I used to joke with him about what he fed his hair, which always got a good laugh. I always liked to believe it was a good balance of proteins and carbohydrates.

He was found by a neighbour, battered and bruised just yards from the safety of his house. Next to him was a large pot of extremely expensive hair pomade with a note attached from the B.G.T.D.L.G.A.D.C

This attack shocked the world. I knew action had to be taken quickly as the B.G.T.D.L.G.A.D.C group were using their negative energy and disregard for peace and harmony to destroy everything I'd been working for.

Assembling my team we worked on pulling out one of our moles from the B.G.T.D.L.G.A.D.C. Like many counter terrorist agencies across the world, we had done our research and found real believers. These were people who were willing to give up ten or twenty years of their life until they were needed.

Naturally most of our recruits had come from the Oxbridge circle back in England, the breeding ground of exceptional talent that far supersedes any other. We had initially tried some prominent US set ups such as Princeton and Yale but we were shocked to find that at least 99.1% of the students had full heads of hair.

That would have to be something to question later, but my initial thought was that the unshakable American confidence would be the reason for such blooming and good looking students.

Our source briefed us on the situation with the B.G.T.D.L.G.A.D.C, especially with regards to the assault on my old friend. It appeared that this attack was just the beginning. They had targeted over 100 more University students who work on the most popular nightclub doors, all of whom had supremely awesome hair.

Whilst I knew what it could be like to be standing in the rain as the beautiful girls were ushered straight to the front of the queue I didn't think that these lush haired men should be punished with physical violence.

After all, if I sported suck locks who knows how different I would have been?

The key was education. We had to stop the recruiting of young and vulnerable kids by the B.G.T.D.L.G.A.D.C. These kids were being brainwashed and some of them still had hair. Our source told us that the group had found a device that could detect male pattern baldness up to five years before it took effect.

This was devastating news as they were no longer restricted to recruiting bald people. They could now plan years in advance.

I have now managed to forge a relationship between my own group and the G.L.B.D where we have reached a mutual agreement to share ALL intelligence as and when it comes in.

By working together we're confident that we can nullify the threat of the B.G.T.D.L.G.A.D.C and increase our understanding of hair related violence. G.L.B.D

Knowing Your Environment

When working undercover, it's hard to predict anything at all but you have to be as prepared as possible. This story is during the time I was working undercover to infiltrate a sleeper cell of the K.A.B.P.

I managed to get invited to a celebratory dinner in one of Berlin's most exclusive restaurants but at the last minute my team were unable to find a suitable wig.

Always prepared to improvise I ran to the shower. Bear in mind, I'm not yet completely bald, but I'm certainly balding, with my fine baby like hair ready to fall out at any given minute. I needed two things.

1. Tresemmé shampoo with B12 Vitamins and Keratin for straw like/brittle hair.
2. Urban Elements molding paste- 'hair thickener that adds definition and volume.'

I was particularly fond of the molding paste which I had discovered in 2003 during a trip to Stockholm, Sweden. It seemed that those Swedes were on to something the world didn't know about. I'm not so sure I'd ever seen this product in any other country.

Combining the Keratin (an extremely strong protein), B12 and the molding paste I was able to turn my straw like hair into a very believable looking head of spiky, normal, medium/thick hair. The only thing I needed now was for the restaurant to have a dim lighting scheme, preferably candles. Have you ever wondered why everyone looks so good in candlelight? Try it for yourself.

Now remember, I'd never met these guys but I knew how dangerous they were. I was acting as an influential banker from Holland who had certain interests in bankrolling the activities of the K.A.B.P. It wouldn't be as easy as that of course, it was necessary for me to meet with them so they could learn a little bit more about me.

Everything was fine as we entered the establishment, and I was pleased with the low level lighting. However, as we were being seated, disaster struck.

There were eight of us, including myself and we had the big table in the far corner of the restaurant. What I immediately noticed was that there was one spot on the table that was perilously placed underneath a lamp.

I could not afford to sit there, no matter how good my cover up was with the Tresemmé and molding paste I knew the lamp would destroy it.

As any thin haired man will tell you, never sit directly under a light. The stronger the light the worse the effect but any light above your head will cut through your hairs like a laser and illuminate your scalp like a theatre spotlight. There is yet to be a solution to the problem, unless you are happy wearing a wig.

"Is there a problem Herman? Perhaps you would prefer a different table?"

Damn. They noticed my discomfort. The next ten seconds would determine whether the operation would be a success or a failure. I chose my words very carefully.

"No problem at all. I just enjoy looking at a table before I sit down to eat."

A forceful grip took hold of my left arm. Hans, one of the more menacing men in the group leaned in close and put his nose to my head taking an enormous sniff. I wondered just how gay we both looked at that moment. He pulled his head back in disgust.

"Keratin!"

The game was over. No thick haired man has any use for Keratin.

But one thing I've always been grateful for is the skill and dedication of the brave men and women who work with me in the background. Without their eyes, ears and bravery, I wouldn't have been able to complete half the missions I've done in my time.

"Down, get down! EVERYBODY DOWN!"

Bursting through every possible entrance and even from the kitchen emerged seven bald men wearing black and armed with 9mm Koch MP5's (a preferred weapon for SWAT teams) and tear gas. Within seconds I was being bundled through the kitchen and out the back door into a waiting Range Rover that sped me off to safety. The mission had failed, but I was still alive.

Blokes And Mirrors

Shamus Baldspotonius- *A condition whereby an individual feels deeply ashamed of his/her bald spot, usually located on the crown of the head.*

All it takes is a fleeting glance. But the ramifications can be huge. For me it all started a year or so after the initial teasing about my hair loss began. I started to become more aware of my problem and as a result I noticed things that before were nothing but dust in the wind.

The dream I have is always the same.

I'm sitting in the barber's comfortable leather chair as he snips away gently at my scalp. There is not really much work for him to do, except for the standard grade two clippers to my back and sides. The same people sit in the background.

There is a clown reading a celebrity magazine, an overweight Chinese man sleeping with drool escaping from a corner of his mouth and a long legged supermodel who has the head of a dog (Labrador).

Towards the end of my haircut I realise what's going on but I'm frozen to the chair unable to move any part of my body. The sheer fear runs through my chest as I try to control my breathing.

The man cutting my hair stops and brushes me down, his eyes slowly turning red. He blows my head with the hairdryer and I feel the icy chill on my bald spot, as cold as death. The hairdresser is laughing now, a laugh which gets stronger each second until he can hardly contain himself.

Blood pours from his mouth, as he spits out the words.

"Time for the mirror baldy-locks!"

I try desperately to move but I can't, and he slowly reaches for the mirror and places it behind my head so I have a full view of the back of my head. There is a huge bald spot there, and I look on in horror.

At this point the Clown, Chinese man and dog headed Supermodel are all standing and staring too, laughing and pointing. The laughter is so powerful it almost tears my ear drums but still I don't wake up.

The last think I see is the impressive selection of hair pomade on the shelf to my right, and I close my eyes and concentrate.

I wake up, coated in a cool layer of sweat, my chest pounding like a jackhammer.

Back in the real world I occasionally caught bald or balding men stealing a last minute glance at me in the street. At first I put it down to my boyish yet slightly dangerous good looks until on closer inspection I realised that the glance was aimed towards my hair.

I concluded that if it was a bald man they were merely recalling a time in their life when they had hair at a similar stage to mine and were no doubt wondering how old I was whilst at the same time predicting just how long I had left before it all fell out.

If it was a man with thinning hair they were simply making a direct comparison, possibly feeling a sense of relief that they were not the only ones out there suffering.

For those of us who are anonymous, particularly me with my double life, it's not so bad. We can afford the luxury of incredibly cool hats and caps that very often make us look better anyway. But it's not all smooth sailing. If you have thinning hair, once the hat goes on it can never come off until bedtime (and even then it's optional). The reason is simple.

The sheer pressure of the hat forces the hair down against the scalp, eventually making it look like someone has put a few sprinkles of straw on your head and tipped a glass of water on top.

Furthermore, for both bald and nearly bald men, if you wear a cap or hat for long enough then in the end the only question going through the heads of everyone (especially potential female partners) is, "I wonder if he's bald?"

If that is the question then they are bound to assume you're embarrassed about it. That's a particular sore point for myself, as I use hats purely on a professional basis. I no longer have the luxury of presenting the real me out there in the open world as years of service have left me with a long list of distinguished enemies.

There are some people who do not have the luxury of disguise. The most obvious example are professional footballers.

Today football has risen to become the most popular global sport, with millions of people from all over the world tuning in to watch the live matches in England, Spain and Italy amongst others.

When you are out there in the middle of the pitch on a rainy night under intense floodlights there is nowhere to hide. The cameras can close in on the top of your head as the rain pelts your bald spot and trickles down over your face like symbolic tears of defeat.

There may even be a super close up of the back of your head, or a slow motion replay that remains on you for an agonisingly long time. All of a sudden seventy million people are aware of your male pattern baldness.

The only man who escaped unscathed from such scrutiny was Zinedine Zidane. His sheer wizardry and unquestionable ability made the baldness completely irrelevant, and to this day he probably remains one of the greatest bald role models we've ever seen.

Back to the subject of mirrors, I can remember a petition that went round a community I belonged to many years ago.

It was lead by a man named Magnus Berthaler who was a well to do lawyer suffering from male pattern baldness. Magnus was enraged by the new three way mirrors that were popping up in every clothes shop on the high street.

Instead of being able to try his clothes on in peace, he was now exposed to multiple angles of his head including the very back which caused him great distress as he had already been diagnosed with Shamus Baldspotonius. The case was dismissed and Magnus passed away seven years later. His wife continues to fight the cause.

Victoria's Secret Party

It's New Years eve. Where would you rather be than New York? As actors leave the sun of Hollywood behind to tread the boards of Broadway, the cops scarf down doughnuts and the Knicks continue to bring in the crowds to Madison Square Garden.

It was on this particular New Years Eve that I saved the hair of over one hundred Victoria's Secret models.

My team and I received our briefing just hours before the planned attack. The after show party not only held the worlds most glamorous girls, but some of the most confident, famous and full haired men ever assembled in just one room.

To loose so much hair would have been a national disaster and one that couldn't happen. But if we couldn't locate the bomb that had been planted then there wasn't going to be much we could do to stop the release of a strain of nerve gas so toxic that not a hair would remain.

The gas had been formulated by a rogue scientist who was familiar to us. Using a complicated mixture of chemicals and with years of funding he was able to create a potent formula.

Releasing one single spray of this gas into a one mile radius could shed all the hairs off three hundred Polar bears.

I briefed my team and told them to ignore the beautiful people and focus on getting the job done. Once we entered the room we would have precisely twenty four minutes locate and diffuse the device.

I spent the first five minutes chatting to a gorgeous Brazilian model who, as it happened, shared a mutual friend with me. I feigned amazement and continued with the job at hand

"Wait. Don't you want to see the cake being cut?"

I turned round and stared at her. What cake. Why were people cutting a cake on New Years Eve?

"Can you take me to this cake please?"

As we walked I called the rest of my team and there was no mistaking it. The bomb had been the centre piece of the party this whole time.

I pulled the plug on the music and took control of the microphone.

"Ladies and gentlemen I apologise for interrupting your night but I am a government agent and I need you all to remain calm, and search your bags for any form of hair wax, gel, paste or pomade."

Within seconds I was being inundated with some of the most colourful and wonderfully smelling hair solutions I'd ever seen in my life. I nearly passed out from the pleasure, but I gathered up the ten most respected brands and got to work, moulding a paste so thick and sticky that it could have been woven by a giant alien Black Widow spider.

"Stand back please."

My team gently smeared the top layer of cream from the cake revealing the blinking device. As a hushed awe came from the crowd I delicately smeared my mixture over the wires and hardware, covering it until there was no sign of danger.

"What do we do now Trey?"

I turned to my Brazilian model.

"We wait."

Even if we tried to run we'd still be caught in the blast radius. I'd either saved everyone or condemned them to a life without hair.

After discussing the state of the economy for around two hours we all decided that the bomb was no longer a threat, so with a sense of sadness, my team and the good looking people trooped out of the building and into the cold New York evening.

The following day I listened with interest to the Mayor's proposition. I understood his gratitude. Despite being humble I knew that what my team and I had accomplished had kept many men and women in business and ensured the security of the fashion industry for a few more years at least.

It was hard to tell just how much effect the credit crunch would have, but I'd heard Warren Buffet's many warnings. However, the Mayor had offered me too much and despite the temptation to bow out in a blaze of glory I knew we weren't done fighting our war.

I politely declined and assured him we would be happy to visit in the near future. And with that, we left the room and vanished into anonymity.

Married Life

It's rare that I get to spend some quality time at home with my family, but when I do, it's the most rewarding experience. That's right. Trey Bald is a married man. It's not something many people know, but I've been attached to my wife Jessica for three years now.

There's also a little Bald scampering around the house too, Trey Jr, who fast approaching his second birthday. They're the two most important people in my life and I owe them both an awful lot, especially as they come second place to my work which is no mean feat.

The key has always been communication, which is something I stress nonstop to my friends who come to me seeking relationship advice.

Jessica has always known that my work comes first and she's been willing to live with that. I don't think there are many people out there so understanding and so sexy at the same time.

At home I prefer to keep things pretty low key. If I'm around I like to get up early at about 6 am and get breakfast ready for Jess and Trey Jr, usually some cereals, juices and scrambled eggs. I'm also proud to say that I make the best coffee, a talent picked up working undercover in Colombia.

Once Jess and I have taken Trey Jr to playschool we go for a gentle jog before returning home to watch Gossip Girl. We're both big fans of the Dan Humphrey character, and I think we both secretly hope Trey

Jr will become exactly like him. What bothers us the most though is wondering how Dan's father, the ex-rock star, not only looks so young and healthy but seems to have a never ending source of money.

My sex life is great and my bald head has always been an aphrodisiac for Jess, something that's common in around thirty percent of women. I guess I got lucky with this one!

If time permits we try to get away once a year to the South of France, where Trey Jr has beaches galore and we have a little time to enjoy each others company away from the hustle and bustle of real life.

I never switch off my secure phone however. Someone with my responsibility doesn't have private time, if that makes sense. If there's a problem, and no one else can deal with it and you know how to find me, then maybe you can call me too.

I met Jess on a routine annual meeting over in Chicago. I've been dealing with the bald community over there for quite sometime now.I try to make it over there once a year to give a speech on baldness and meet the people over the course of a weekend. Jess was working at one of these functions behind the bar.

When I met her she was an aspiring actress but was struggling with the current climate. She spoke of moving to New York to give it a serious go but something in her voice told me she was looking for more. Later that night I told her I was going make her my wife and she laughed in my face.

It would be nice to think that one day I could give all this bald crap up and return home for good, maybe working as a carpenter. Unfortunately I don't see the world coming together anytime soon.

Just like no one will ever stop terrorism or racism, no one will ever really manage to put a stop to bald related violence but that is why I'm out there each and every day handling my business.

Groupie Therapy

When you're a bald superstar your life doesn't exactly follow the usual white picket fence and apple pie routine.

I don't get home from work at seven, to a hot dinner and a smiling wife. I mean, I get home and my wife smiles, but it's just not as often as I'd like. Now that I have a kid too, things have changed.

So why do my female fans, or as I like to call them, groupies, still write and ask me what they can do with their bald husbands to spice things up a little in the bedroom. Well, I talked it over with Jess and I've been given the green light.

My love is like an art form. Once it's out there it doesn't belong to me, it belongs to everyone and I want to see you getting the very best sex out of your sex life.

When Jess and I first met, she wasn't initially attracted to my lack of hair.

Things got even worse when it fell out in its entirety and that's when the arguments started. She was often confused with my winning personality and impressive physique but it just wasn't enough for her.

Luckily for me though, Jess had fallen in love with Trey Bald so instead of being kicked to the curb we worked together to solve our problems. Here are just a few of our creative ideas.

Lesson # 1. People are more attractive when you're drunk.

One Friday night, Jess and I went out to talk about my baldness and discuss some of the measures that we could take to move past it. After a few beers, the atmosphere had became sensationally and seductively relaxed and we opted to liven things up with a round of tequila slammers. Not one to shy away from a complete bender I ordered a tray of tequila shots and lined them up. That was when Jess took control.

"Wait. Lean forward. I want to use your bald head."

Jess sprinkled a neat line of salt on the left hand side of my dome and squeezed some lemon over on the right hand side.

Despite the mild amounts of citric acid in my eye I have to say that it was a great feeling to feel my future wife tongue the top of my chrome dome and get wasted at the same time. It was almost as if my baldness was making the magic in the room that night.

Lesson # 2. Your hands are so soft.

Nope. That's my head sweetheart.

For our first anniversary I took Jess to an all day beauty spa. You know the type of place. Mud baths, mineral juices, aloe vera injections and so on.

When it was time for her massage, I sneaked quietly into the dim room that was playing Sigur Ros and winked at Jurgen the well toned club masseuse. Jurgen took his cue and tip toed to the cupboard in the corner to pull out the tub of melted Toblerone (toblerone is a triangular chocolate bar with some form of nut in it. You can find out more on Google).

With Jurgen's help I smeared the chocolate goo on my head until it was completely covered and then I got to work on my wife.

Using my head like a painter uses his brush I swept with care and patience on the canvas that was Jess.

She let out sounds that I've never heard before, certainly not in another human being.

There was so much love in the room that I even allowed Jurgen to stay and watch, but never for one minute did I consider inviting him to join in. That's just not something that interests Trey Bald.

To cut a long story short, it was messy, delicious and witnessed by a young and healthy German man. If that's not alternative then I just don't know what is.

Lesson # 3. Ladies love Frank Sinatra.

If you've got a beautiful voice but you're spending those long weekend nights sitting on your own watching television then you're a fool. Unless you're watching Gossip Girl, Supernatural or something similar (run of the mill American tv) then you have no excuse not to be romancing an exotic or altogether ordinary girl.

I know what you're thinking. With all my other abilities surely I can't claim to sing like Frank Sinatra as well? I'm afraid not, life's not all peaches and cream. In fact, I compare my singing ability to a guinea pig being strangled. So how can you work round this? It's easier than you think.

Once a month for the last two years Jess and I have enjoyed a night of fine wine and singing in the privacy of our own home.

Using a website I don't wish to name in this book for security reasons (as always) I'm able to hire a multitude of look-a-like singers.

There's a Frank, a Stevie Wonder, a Michael Jackson and an Anthony Keidis amongst others. With a choice of over one hundred you're easily able to find the right style for you.

We normally use Frank but every now and then it's fun to push the boundaries and go with something controversial like Chris Cornell (who we both admire on a technical level even if he wouldn't be an obvious choice for some couples).

The process is simple. The singer turns up at the house and remains in the living room gargling water to warm up and possibly enjoying a cigar or two if we're going for the whole husky gravel voice thing.

After an hour or two, when Jess and I have finished our polite conversation and gourmet meal, the singer is allowed to join us in the room.

Then comes the bald value. Jess paints my head just like a microphone, something she really enjoys doing. When everything is dry, the singer can perform but only by singing into my bald head, and under no circumstances is he or she allowed to look at Jess.

The only eye contact comes from Trey Bald.

The real lesson here is to be creative with your bald head. Of course there's a high chance your other half would prefer the crunchy locks of your neighbour but that's no excuse to throw in the towel and concede defeat.

Alcohol is a definite help as well, but not too much. Just enough to numb the part of the brain that picks up on baldness.

Champagne Brings The Pain

What most people never knew was that I spent a short period of time held as a prisoner in a castle right in the centre of Florence which I recommend as a wonderful place to visit if you're going to Italy. The streets are winding and cobbled, and it doesn't seem like anyone is actually ever doing anything, unless it's making you a coffee.

On this particular trip I was researching the possibility of opening up operations with a similar Italian agency that has since been disbanded due to multiple security breaches.

I was enjoying a gelato when I was snatched right off the street in broad daylight. I believe it was a pistachio and cookie dough cone but I'm not so sure about the cookie dough part.

It's more likely I picked something similar with a different name but with eight hundred and sixty seven choices and the trauma you're about to read you can understand why my memory of the ice cream is a little hazy.

I'd only enjoyed a few mouthfuls when a young and strong looking man delivered an excruciating blow to my kidney before another two men threw me into the back of a pizza delivery van.

My first reaction was disappointment. There were no pizzas, and although this wasn't a social call I had always wanted to try an authentic Italian pizza.

"Welcome to Italy, Mr. Bald."

I didn't recognise the man in front of me holding the gun but he had a familiar demeanour about him.

It was almost like he wasn't good at normal things in life but he'd somehow found a shortcut to success, judging by the impressively cut suit he wore. He was extremely average looking to the trained eye, although your normal man or woman on the street would have considered him quite slick.

Trey Bald is not just any man however.

"Please, call me Trey. And you are?"

The man looked amused. The other two laughed mockingly.

"So many questions."

"That's the first one I've asked."

Everyone fell silent. They knew I had a point.

As the van came to a stop I was blindfolded and frog marched up a never ending flight of stairs, and judging by the echo it was a castle of some sort.

After having my blindfold removed, I was ruthlessly thrown into the corner of an empty stone walled room and the door was slammed shut with an almighty bang.

I tried to remember what Frank Abagnale did in 'Catch me if you Can' but I immediately became embroiled in a debate as to whether I should think about the film or the book. The book was much better so I chose that, but I struggled to recall the details of his cramped cell in Perpignan (I think it was Perpignan).

A few hours later I was given a pair of brand new diesel jeans, a crisp and funky shirt and an optional baseball cap. I was then escorted to an adjacent room where I was placed on a comfortable leather couch and handed a chilled glass of Krug non-vintage.

I asked the man what was going on but he didn't reply. It was interesting to notice how he shared the same characteristics as his leader. Not that good looking but well dressed, and a slightly undeserved element of arrogance. Five minutes later he was replaced by a scantily clad blonde woman who screamed sex appeal.

I'll leave out the long and arduous details but we spent hours talking and listening to Fall Out Boy as I got more and more drunk. I definitely felt a connection, until she slowly handcuffed me.

That's when I felt more than a connection, that's when I felt it was Trey Bald time.

She took of my cap and stepped back in disgust at my bald head. Something felt wrong, and through my drunken and lust filled haze I suddenly realised what it was.

This was an extremely old school method of torture, leading an individual into a false sense of security before taking it all away, breaking the captive until he/she just can't take it anymore and divulges all the important information.

I knew I was right when the blonde started pointing and laughing. I'd be lying if I said I wasn't very disappointed but I was more angry at myself for thinking this was going to be my lucky night. There was only one thing for it. *Hairnergy.*

I focused all of my anger, mostly revolving around the fact I wasn't going to get to sleep with this woman and I looked down at the ground waiting for her to come too close. I felt and absorbed her mocking laughter and numerous cries of

"Bald old man, bald old man, bald old man!"

Then she made her first mistake.

Leaning down to whisper another bald insult into my ear she was caught off guard as I let out a primeval cry of war, breaking through the handcuffs as if they were made from Haribo. I took control of the girl in seconds and we were off down the stairs in search of an exit.

The leader looked shocked as I entered what appeared to be his study, holding the blonde in front of me, my right hand poised above her head clutching the now empty bottle of champagne.

"Mr. Bald, it seems you may have outstayed your welcome."

He reached for the button on his desk. He was wasting his time.

"I've disabled the alarm system. No one will be coming tonight. Now tell me what you want or I'm going to smash this beautiful face open with the bottle."

I desperately hoped he would believe me because to this day I have never, and never will, hit a lady.

"Just relax. I'm your friend. I'm here to help you succeed in life."

What the hell did that mean? I tried to put the pieces together. He didn't look inspiring, but he acted in a manner that suggested he was more important than Nelson Mandela.

Suddenly it clicked. How could I have been so stupid?

"I know you. You're Regis Clarke, head of the BIE."

I knew by his reaction I was right. The BIE, otherwise known as Brilliant Internet Entrepreneurs, are a group that uncover extremely niche markets in order to assemble the information into an easy to read e-book which they then sell online.

Their brilliant PPC (pay per click marketing), SEO (search engine optimisation) and other online marketing skills enable them to build up an extremely loyal following and a consistently high level of sales. There wasn't much they hadn't written (or had an e-book written for them) about.

I also knew that they had taken me hostage to try and gain as much information as possible on male pattern baldness. How ironic that I would be writing a book myself.

"Tell me something Regis, do you know what I mean by Hairnergy?"

Regis looked puzzled.

Internet entrepreneurs are not used to being wrong, confused or unaware of anything in the world.

I pushed the blonde girl away and at a safe distance and focused myself on the man in front of me.

Looking down at the ground I recalled the initial shame I felt when I lost my hair and combined it with the time I studied an e-book on hair re-growth that never worked but cost me over twenty British pounds.

Regis began to look worried. That's when he heard the roar, and his worry became a paralysing and unforgettable fear of the like he'd never known before.

I lunged forward hitting him with the power of a juggernaut at full speed, taking him crashing through the stone wall and down thirty metres to the damp grass on the outside of the castle.

I knew he was dead on impact but I didn't have time to clear up this mess.

Who knows how many of his associates could have been listening in on Skype or MSN Messenger (using the audio or video call), and he may have even tapped a quick SOS message using his I-phone.

I noticed a folded e-book with the title 'Ultimate tips for chatting up women', and thrust it in my pocket just in case. Then I was gone, disappearing into the winding street amongst the bustling and gesticulating public of Florence.

Nightclubs

Part of my research has always been dedicated to conducting real life tests, as all the laboratory work and theorising in the world comes a distant second to observing real life situations.

I have always been convinced that sub consciously or consciously bald people are viewed as lesser people. Whether this is fair or not is not the question. The question is why? Why are we programmed to think this way?

A test I developed a few years ago involved the use of subjects in nightclub queues across central London. Since then I have managed to post people to nightclubs all over the world, and the results have always been the same.

- The trendier/swankier/more expensive the nightclub, the less bald men that gained entrance. Only seven percent of bald males were admitted into such nightclubs from 2000-2009. Don't believe me? Swing by my office sometime.

I was astounded at some of the figures that were sent back to me and decided to enter the playing field myself.

I usually don't have time for minor operations such as this as I'm far too busy risking life and limb in more precarious situations, but every now and then I like to remind myself what it is like to conduct simple tasks.

After all, it is the research from the most basic exercises that creates the foundations for greater future discoveries.

At the time of this operation, labelled "Don't you know who I am?" I was in Sydney, Australia which meant that there was only one place for me to visit.

The Ivy bar has been described as a sophisticated new urban playground unlike anything Sydney has ever seen before.

Owned by Justin Hemmings, the country's greatly admired entrepreneur, The Ivy prides itself on its sensational décor and staff who are extremely easy on the eye.

As I neared the front of the queue the first visual notes I made were that the two bouncers on the door were ugly, and the girl with the guest list wasn't really much better.

I was immediately told that I had to be on the guest list, and the girl was even backed up by an extremely trendy young man in shorts who sported a spray tan that a British teenage girl would be proud of. Of course it wasn't so much the spray tan or his khaki shorts that scared me as much as the menacing and beautiful hair on his head.

I thought immediately of my poor friend back at University who had suffered such a savage beating when all he was doing was sharing his hair with the world.

"Never mind. Maybe another night."

"Thank you sir. Enjoy your evening."

It was another typical bit of foreplay that plays out between bald men and guest list holders all over the world every weekend.

I slipped away into the darkness and located my teams' van a couple of blocks away. Climbing in the back, I reported on events as they took notes and input data on to the computer. As I spoke I slipped on the finest wig that money can buy.

By the time I'd made the fine adjustments I looked like Harry Kewell but with even thicker hair. It was unbeatable.

"Welcome to The Ivy sir, I hope you have a pleasant night."

And I got a smile too. If I didn't know any better I'd say the guest list girl planned on making my night as pleasant as possible.

Gliding up the stairs without attracting attention I found a glass of chilled champagne, Krug non-vintage (the finest) and found a spot on the dance floor where I elegantly swayed whilst secretly filming the unsuspecting masses with my wireless mini color spy camera (including receiver and accessories).

The live feed went straight back to my team in the van, and they were able to store the footage and ensure its potential use for future presentations.

Just as I was about to leave I noticed a group of extremely successful looking men in suits. They were being ushered into a private room by an exquisite blonde woman who ran her hand through their hair one by one as they entered.

Once they were all inside the blonde resumed her duty monitoring the club and for a split second I thought she'd made me until I noticed there was a fat pony tailed man throwing up in the swimming pool to my right. The perfect distraction.

I wasted no time in moving towards the door of the private room. I knew what I had to do and there was no time for sophisticated equipment.

I burst through the door, stumbling like a drunken fool looking for somewhere to urinate.

"Heeeeeeey, isshshhh this the mensss room?"

The men jumped up in unison before their leader barked at me.

"Strewth mate, who the bloody hell are you? Get out!"

I apologised and clumsily turned round to leave the room. I had seen all I needed. It may have only been a fleeting glance but the projector had made a fairly clear picture on the wall. The picture was of me. I don't know how they got it, or where it was taken. Possibly Israel. But the headline above the picture was what scared me the most.

Priority target.

Why I Hate A Sales Call In The Morning

Just before ten a.m. on a fantastic Australia summer's day I lay by the pool enjoying my cup of freshly brewed Early Grey breakfast tea. You've probably worked out that this was the morning after my trip to The Ivy where I uncovered a plot to have me killed.

Hearing that someone hates you is always a gut wrenching feeling, no matter how well you disguise it. I can remember a time in the playground at school when a girl decided to pass on the information that her best friend Connie hated me and it didn't feel good at all.

Knowing that someone wants to kill you is less traumatic. Your survival instinct overpowers any other emotion.

As I turned over on to my front to ensure I had an equal tan on my back, the mobile phone rang.

"Hello, is that Trey Bald?"

An unsecure line. Who could this be?

"My name's Daniel and I'm calling you from Westpac as a follow up to the letter we sent you that entitles you to our new life insurance policy."

Westpac? Life insurance? Policy? Something didn't add up.

"I don't have a Westpac account," I responded.

The salesman went silent. I heard the faint sound of a click on the line, and that was when I saw the fraction of light glinting off the edge of the deck chair just to the right of my head. A trap.

I rolled and simultaneously swung the deckchair up to protect me. The first bullet tore through the chair's material like a knife through hot butter and I realised that my actual bullet proof deck chair was still being repaired up in Brisbane.

The second bullet tore into my right leg, just above the knee. I grunted in pain but managed to block it enough to drag myself inside the glass doors and to the safety of the downstairs bar I'd had installed.

I was low on ideas. Without a weapon or any hair products all I could rely on was reflecting the sun off my bald spot, but now I was inside the house like a sitting duck.

I thought of Jess and Trey Jr, and all the wonderful people I'd served with.

My day dream was interrupted by a giant cracking sound followed by a thud. I couldn't believe my luck. The sniper had fallen out of the tree. Did I plant that tree with weak branches on purpose? Probably not, but it was a good idea for future sniper attacks.

I hauled myself as quick as I could out on to the grass, leaving a thin trail of blood behind me from my leg wound. The sniper looked immobilised, a possible broken leg. I managed to heave myself on top of him for questioning.

"Why won't Justin Hemmings let me in The Ivy? Is it because I'm bald? Is he the man who sent you here?"

The sniper gathered his breath and stared up at me. I knew the eyes of a killer when I saw one. Everything about him was alive, except for those eyes.

"You have no idea what's going on. Justin Hemmings has nothing to do with anything."

"The why can I never get into The Ivy?"

The sniper looked frustrated.

"You can't just turn up to a place like The Ivy. You have to add something. Bring some girls or at least dress well. And of course you can't be bald you moron. It's one of the best clubs in the world."

I wasn't going to get any answers out of him. This man was a professional. A professional who made the mistake of having killer hair. Quite literally.

I grabbed a hold of his thick blonde locks and stuffed them over his face, pushing down with all my might. If he'd had a clean army crew cut then I probably would have died that morning.

I rolled off the dead sniper and called the one man I could trust within the vicinity.

Super Rob was a local musician who played a mix of down right depressing music and catchy pop songs. I'd met him in London years earlier and always tried to show up whenever he played a gig. For now, he was my only option. My own team could have been compromised, how else did my enemies find me so quickly.

"Trey, how's it going man?"

He sounded happy.

"Super Rob. I've got one dead body and I've taken a hit to the leg."

"I'll be there in five minutes. Apply pressure to the wound."

He hung up and I lay on my back, drenched in the powerful sun. It must have been at least thirty degrees. I hadn't had a chance to put any sun cream on my head either.

I rested up back at Super Rob's studio apartment and forgot about my troubles with a few beers and a thai take away. We both decided that things had become a bit too hot for me, and maybe it was time to retreat home for a while.

That was the beauty of how I worked. With such a loyal team that remains nameless (leaving me with all the credit) I can afford to simply disappear for as long as is necessary. This not only confuses the enemy but makes them paranoid, which is when they are most likely to make a mistake.

Before boarding my flight back to England I promised Super Rob that I'd give music a go as soon as I had a chance. He left me with some inspirational words.

"Music's a source. It'll change your life man."

He was probably right.

I'm Sorry Jimmy

The closest friend I've ever had was Jimmy.

Jimmy and I met in school, we took the same Chemistry class. He was always on the fat side and the other boys never let him forget it. That was until I showed up.

You see, I moved around a lot of schools in my youth due to my parents working in the Foreign Office.

When we settled in New York (little did I know it would be the setting for mine and Jess' beloved Gossip Girl). I was finally about to make my first real friend.

On my opening day I was ten minutes late for Chemistry class following a hair modelling assignment that had run a little longer than expected. Naturally, when I breezed in apologetically, no one quite had the guts to make any wise cracks and I couldn't blame them as my hair, quite frankly, looked superb.

But there was one kid who wasn't getting it quite as easy. He was sitting at the front, with a shock of red curly hair and love handles that protruded from his shirt. Poor guy, I couldn't imagine what it must have been like for him.

Every time the teacher turned around, some punk from the back of the room would fire a paper pellet with an elastic band. That may not sound like much, but those pellets can draw blood, believe me. I felt awful, but I wasn't sure what to do.

When I saw the first tear escape down his chubby little cheek I had my answer.

I marched across the playground looking for him. The kid was called Zack Mackchops and he was the ringleader.

Like all clever bullies he hung out with a big crowd and none of them ever smiled.

"Excuse me. It's Zack right?"

The circle opened up and I was only yards away from him. He looked surprised. But then you would be surprised if the new kid in school was marching towards you holding a medium to large sized moist trout.

I revolved my right arm three hundred and sixty degrees and brought the trout down on the top of his head with an awe inspiring slap.

His eyes rolled and his knees buckled. As he lay on the ground in a state of shock and intense pain I made sure there was no room for misunderstanding.

"He may be ginger, he may be fat and he may have love handles but let me tell you something right now. If I ever see you picking on Jimmy again, I will find an even bigger and fresher trout to slap your face with."

And with that, I had my first best friend. I didn't know that so many years later, this moment would seal Jimmy's fate.

It was shortly after my escapades at the Victoria's Secret party that I heard the news. But it was the people who claimed responsibility that shocked me the most.

A group that I'd assumed was a rumour, a group so ridiculous I never once took any intel on them seriously. My colleagues had repeatedly tried to persuade me otherwise but I never budged.

Stupid Trey Bald

Stupid Trey Bald (S.T.B) formed sometime between 1997 and 2001 but it's been near impossible to pinpoint the exact date.

The group was believed to be an initial reaction to my modelling days but it's not clear whether my new found status as a Counter Baldsim agent has been a factor.

The cops found Jimmy face down in a Vanilla milkshake, his favourite. But there were two things that made the crime chilling to me.

First of all they'd managed to fit his head perfectly into the milkshake container, which is hardly big enough for my hand.

Secondly, there was graffiti all over Jimmy's apartment. The message was loud and clear.

I guess if he ate more trout he wouldn't be such a fat fuck.

Of all the people in the world to form the S.T.B group I'd never considered Zack Mackchops as a suspect.

It's just like I tell my team every day at work. Nothing is as it seems. Jimmy was the only friend I had away from work and my family.

Zack Mackchops had started a dangerous game.

I called everyone I knew in New York, until I worked out that Jimmy was the only person I knew. Not one to give up, I called everyone I knew in New Jersey and within the hour I had a plan and a team ready to go.

My usual guys wouldn't be involved in this one, after all, it wasn't hair related. This was personal.

As I grabbed my bag and headed to the front door, I was more than surprised to see a police car outside with officers advancing up my driveway.

Jessica and Trey Jr were away at their Aunts house which was a relief but I still had no idea what was going on. I opened the door to greet them but as it turned out there were no greetings necessary.

"Trey Bald you're under the arrest for the murder of Jimmy Lubberwick. You do not have to say anything but anything you do say may be used against you in the court of law. Do you understand?"

I understood just fine. I understood that Zack Mackchops was a dead man walking.

The End Of Counter Baldism

The cell was humble, but then it was the first time I'd seen the inside of one. I'd been locked up here for two days now without a phone call and I knew something was wrong. I didn't understand how it was possible for me to be flown out to LA when there were plenty of well kept prisons in Britain. My instinct told me I wasn't safe, but there was nowhere else to go. So I stayed calm.

It wasn't easy, I already knew what kind of animals I was living with in this hell hole. For starters the dumb ass guards had put me in cell block H which was home to the notorious Razor twins, members of the S.T.B (Stupid Trey Bald) group and loyal to their leader, Zack Mackchops.

Mackchops was the reason I was in here, of that I was sure, but I didn't realise he'd followed this move with a second punch. He'd planned the whole thing, and god knows how long he'd been preparing for the day.

Now I'd been hung out to dry, left to the sharks, thrown to the dogs. I wouldn't be able to avoid the recreation time in the yard and that would be when the Razor twins would make their attack.

I knew some of the guards were on the S.T.B payroll so knowing who I could talk to or trust was becoming increasingly difficult.

"Mr. Bald. Time to stretch your legs."

The guard had broken my concentration. I looked up at him and searched for any familiar signs but I found none.

This guy could have been a loving husband who plays baseball with his son in the garden or a monstrous paedophile and proud member of the S.T.B. group. I thought about the fight or flight theory.

I could not afford to be seen as a weakling in this prison.

"Sure thing boss. Just one question though. What colour paint did you guys use for the ceiling?"

The split second was all I needed. As the guards eyes instinctively flicked up I charged catching him right in the stomach with my head.

The sheer lack of hair meant that the blow was delivered with the force of a shot gun. The pair of us were on the floor in the main corridor but I was quick as a cat. Jumping to my feet I caught the dazed guard with a fierce kick to the head, and followed this up with a devastating stamp on to his rib cage.

The sound of the crack was enough for me to know he wouldn't be getting up. Inmates all around rattled at their cell bars and screamed profanities at me.

I saw the throng of guards in riot gear approaching me and immediately dropped to the floor and tried to make myself as small as possible as the blows from their clubs came raining down on me like a fair ground game of hit the hedgehog.

An hour later and I found myself sitting on the other side of the desk to an intimidating man called Raymond Strickland. Mr. Strickland ran the entire prison, and I'd heard a lot of stories about him in my brief time behind bars.

"The guard you beat up was two days away from retirement. He has a sick wife, two kids in college and he donates half his wages to various charities every year. You might also be interested to know that when he's not working, he runs a youth centre for disadvantaged inner city children. It's unpaid work but he simply refuses to let those kids down. I believe he's taken over five thousand youths off the dangerous street and into the workforce since 2005."

No regrets Trey, you did the right thing. Anyone else and it could have been you in hospital. That's what I kept telling myself. I felt sorry for the heroic guard but I still needed to figure out why I was here.

"That's fascinating Mr. Strickland. Now can I call my lawyer?"

If looks could kill I'd be dead ten times over. But looks can't kill and Strickland knew it. I didn't believe he was a part of the conspiracy, just an old timer who had no idea that his values had long been rejected by the next generation of men looking to make a fast buck.

"Mr. Bald, I've dealt with people like you before. People who consider themselves above the law. They think the rules shouldn't have to apply to them. But believe me slaphead, they do. So, before I go I just want to make one thing clear."

"I'm all ears Strickland," I responded, unwilling to be phased by this verbal attack.

"One day you *will* be taken down. Maybe not today, tomorrow or next month. But you will be taken down Mr. Bald and when you are, I'll be there."

All of a sudden Mr. Strickland grinned. A cold and evil looking grin. It was as though Satan had just landed in his thick set body. He leaned close, so close that his lips touched my right ear.

I could smell his stale breath. It smelt like old ham and spearmint.

Then he uttered his final words before leaving the room.

"Mr. Mackchops is a very persistent man. I wish you all the best."

Son of a bitch I thought, staring in amazement as Mr. Strickland left the room. Was there anyone that Mackchops couldn't buy?

I didn't have time to dwell on that thought as another man entered. A man I knew very well on a professional level.

It was Johnny Dynamite, the leader of the world.

Most people are led to believe that the leader of the free world is the President of the United States.

They also believe that the Prime Minister and his backroom staff control England.

In fact, we all believe many things in life. Whether it's UFO's, the existence of a passive Polish man or that children can see dead people- we all believe something. Well there was one thing I knew for sure.

Long before man had landed on the moon and the founding of Mcdonalds, there existed a committee so secret that some of its members didn't even know they were members.

This committee is responsible for appointing the leader of the entire world, regardless of race, religion or looks. I should point out that there has *never* been a bald leader of the world, but maybe that's because the right person always happened to have hair.

Captain Johnny Dynamite was a typical appointment. I wasn't going to argue. He stood at just over 6 feet tall, with broad shoulders and a winning smile that was protected by prominent cheek bones that were nearly bigger than the pair on Johnny Depp.

He ate mostly pasta and fruit, and listened to a lot cool music like Mos Def and The Pharcyde.

He was currently sleeping with two women, sometimes at the same time, and living in a sweet pad somewhere in Europe. To simplify it for you, Johnny Dynamite was the man. And now he was standing in front of me.

"Trey Bald. Never thought I'd be seeing you under these circumstances."

I didn't answer. You don't talk to Captain Johnny Dynamite. He talks to you.

"The corruption in this place goes far Trey, but not far enough for me to pay you back for all the work you've done for me. You'll be leaving here in two hours. I've put you on a flight to the safest place on earth, Hollywood. When you get there, you do what you want but I have to ask you a favour Trey."

I looked up at Captain Dynamite.

"I want you to end your operations Trey. Consider your group disbanded. I have informed your partners. I know you've dedicated many years to fighting hair related terrorism and for that I'm sorry. But it has to be done, and I don't expect to hear from you again."

And with that, my life had changed. Captain Dynamite flicked a cigarette into his mouth, flicked open his Zippo and inhaled deeply. He had style alright.

"You still banging that girl Jessica?"

"She's my wife sir."

Captain Dynamite smiled.

"Good. I like her. I'm sure you'll miss her a lot. She's smoking hot Trey, I'm proud of you. Look after yourself."

Captain Johnny Dynamite turned and walked out of the room, along with the rest of my life as I knew it.

He'd saved me, but at what cost? I relaxed knowing that I would live to see the next day. A new guard escorted me to my room to collect up my few belongings.

I was off to Hollywood.

My New Life

The last person who expected a record contract was me. I knew my singing ability was very limited but I couldn't understand why this fact kept me awake night after night.

My problem is that I just can't accept not being the best at anything, so you can imagine how complicated this is when my son has a table tennis tournament with his school friends.

I have had many a falling out due to the Trey Bald competitive nature. But at the end of the day, if you're born to win, it's as simple as that. God took my hair, and I'm taking your pride.

In the aftermath of Jimmy's death, I needed something else in my life. All Counter Baldism operations were officially dead and I spent hours alone trying to find myself emotionally.

I had left Jessica and Trey Jr behind, unsure of when I would see them again. It was then that I picked up a guitar and felt something new.

To this day I can't tell you what it was, but it was a little like that feeling you get when your Chinese take away finally arrives at the door. A mix of adrenalin and excitement, followed by a slight pang in your stomach.

The following day I hired Christina Loosenseduce, a very well known singing coach. Christina had worked with the likes of Axl Rose, Stevie Wonder and Nick Lachey.

I had to spend all of Jess' savings just to gain her services for a week. It was money well spent because a week is all a quick learner needs.

For eight hours a day, Christina and I sat in a smart room in Beverly Hills and worked on my voice and other things. It was a bizarre seven days and emotions ran high, most notably on the secure private line (courtesy of Captain Dynamite) with Jess who wasn't happy about who I'd hired to help me.

She had every right to be concerned, Christina and I enjoyed hours of intense and very physical sex but I must stress that it was nothing more than an essential release for me following the tragedy of Jimmy. I always have and always will love Jess more than anything in this world.

Using a little of Trey Jr's college fund I wasted no time in assembling the band. I hand picked the guys who I knew had both an eclectic style and the right attitude. We agreed on a band name almost straight away.

Bald 172

Trey Bald- Lead Guitar/Vocals

Super Rob- Rhythm Guitar/Vocals

Mad Mike- Bass

Cup Man- Drums

We'd spent most of our money on renting a house in the Hollywood Hills and the top of the range studio equipment which meant that we couldn't afford a top Producer.

We were also unknown as a band so it seemed logical not to waste time trying to work with someone like Rick Rubin and instead I hired an upcoming young lad called Nathan Nerdanté to produce the album.

Nathan was a student studying Computer Science but he had a great and varied taste in music not to mention a natural ability with the technical side of things. I'd met him at the cinema on one of those nights where I'd just wanted to be by myself. Fate is a funny thing.

The first few days of recording were tough.

Super Rob was having trouble with his stomach following a badly made pizza and I couldn't hit my vocals.

Cup Man laid down all of his drum parts in forty eight hours, the guy was a machine.

Mad Mike was fine but there wasn't much he could do without Super Rob and myself performing at one hundred percent.

Nathan suggested that we needed to adopt a different style, less heavy metal and more pop punk. He then had a little dig at my vocals, claiming they needed some work. I thought this was unprofessional to say the least as I'd been working myself into the ground trying to get it right.

I took Nathan out into the garden and gave him the beating of a lifetime. As I drove him to hospital I made it clear that although I admired his work ethic and commitment, I would not be spoken to in such a way, especially by a student who didn't have many friends.

We put our problems firmly behind us and the following day we all got down to work.

The next week was intense.

I uncovered all the emotions that were buried deep inside me from the death of Jimmy, to my years of undercover ops fighting some of the most evil people in the world.

Mad Mike was killing the bass and Super Rob and I harmonised like we'd been playing together for fifty years.

Nathan Nerdanté spent hours mixing and producing the goods just like Michael Carrick does every weekend in England.

I wasn't sure where Cup Man was but he had a girlfriend in town so I assumed he was getting some of the good stuff. We had a platinum album on the way.

At the end of the week (Friday morning) I got a phone call from Cup Man who was in trouble with some local hoods that were holding him and his girlfriend at gun point.

I left the house in Mad Mike's drop top sports car and stuck on 'Ug' by Mr. Scruff at full blast. Sipping on my mango smoothie I enjoyed the sun drenching my pale face. I'd spent too long stuck in the house recording the album, and now I was going to exercise that deep urge for destruction.

I've fought every Johnny Bigtime out there, from London to Brazil, a couple of local hoodlums from the street didn't worry me at all. I even made a call to Nathan en route to discuss which track we should release as the first single. I was relaxed. Never better.

As it turned out, Cup Man had been trying to score some weed when the mood turned sour. One of the gang had taken a shine to his girl and this hadn't gone down well with him. Not well at all.

I know how a man can get when it comes to love so I opted for a little caution just in case things had escalated. My training from years gone by had kicked in like a chilli high and I was on auto-pilot.

I rounded the corner, parking behind a construction site before making my way through the alley to where the danger awaited.

I could see Cup Man and his girl locked in their Range Rover whilst a gang of four men circled dangerously like sharks in the open water.

This was bad. Right in broad daylight.

In all the excitement of the music I'd practically forgotten about my baldness. Being bald in Hollywood is not an option. It's the land of the famous and beautiful, and even if you're not famous you're working on being famous so a full head of hair is a must. It wasn't long before the inevitable happened.

"Yo! Get the fuck out of dodge you bald ass motherfucker!"

A group of rich and confident teenagers had spotted me from their shiny Ferrari and they had blown my cover. Turning in unison, the gang of four men advanced on me. I made a snap decision.

"Drive Cup Man, drive!"

Cup Man sped off, leaving me to my fate. I hoped he was heading to the studio, he'd been away for some important sessions and I wanted his opinion on some of the mixing.

"Jesus man, he is bald! That's some sick shit."

Of course.

Not only do bald people face a life of isolation in Hollywood, they also make the other normal guys and girls feel scared. I'd heard stories about how male pattern baldness was perceived as an illness in Hollywood, no different from catching a common cold.

In general, those with thick hair ensured that they kept a firm distance from anyone with thinning or bald hair for fear of catching it themselves and seeing their own dreams flush down the toilet. Assuming that these men were aspiring actors I lowered my head down like a bull and charged.

"I'm contagious, I'm contagious!"

With a mixture of screams and shouts, the men dispersed in separate directions, tripping and bumping into each other, desperate to escape.

It felt good to resolve something without using violence.

Suddenly, I'd never been happier about the end of my Counter Baldism days.

Announcing The Album

On a cool summer's night, we all sat outside on the lawn and prepared to announce Bald 172 to the world. Our first album was called, 'You Can Keep Your Hair For All I Care."

Nathan prepared the steaks and chicken, Mad Mike watched over the beers and I sat by the pool with Super Rob and Cup Man, debating on who to hire as our PR guru.

Before all that though, there were six pretty obvious questions that needed to be answered:

1. What would be our single?
2. Should we get a Myspace profile?
3. Should we get a group going on Facebook?
4. Should we get a group going on BEBO?
5. Should we get something on Friends Reunited?
6. Should we get something on Twitter?

We all knew what the single had to be. It was the reason we were here in the first place and the whole reason my life had taken a complete U-turn towards music.

Jimmy. To honour his memory I chose 'Death by Milkshake' to be the first Bald 172 single.

As for the internet, I left all that to Nathan Nerdanté. He was up to date with all the trends and micro trends and his programming ability would enable us to create far funkier profiles than the other bands out there.

The plan was simple. Once we had an online presence, we would find some form of spamming software and add everyone on the internet as our friends. Then, the word of mouth would happen and we'd become one of the best bands in the world.

After eating our food, we tossed a coin to decide on who should handle our PR.

If it was heads we would turn to Maia Celeste who was well known for her work on the Obama campaign, and tails would be Ted Bogus who had run two wildly unsuccessful PR campaigns for a couple of college bands.

The coin landed on tails and I retreated to my temporary office to give Ted a call and see if he would be available for an immediate start.

That Monday we all sat down in Ted's office, which doubled as a dentist waiting room in North Hollywood. The first thing he told me was that I could not be the face of the band. I asked why.

"No offence Trey. But you're bald. Bald doesn't sell records."

I knew he was right but I wasn't willing to let go of my status. I left Ted with an ultimatum.

Either he worked with us using me as the face of the band or he went back to doing chores for teenagers playing out of their parents' garage.

We were a serious outfit with a strong internet presence and enough money to rent a house in the hills. If he couldn't make that work then I didn't know what all the effort was for.

The following week, after a solid seven days celebrating the completion of our debut album, 'You can keep your hair for all I care', we drove out to West Hollywood for our first bit of publicity.

Ted met us at the location, a small supermarket that sold predominantly Korean food. It had been hard work but at the least minute Ted had arranged for us to declare the new aisle seven (which would stock mostly noodles and rice) open.

A lot of other bands would have turned their nose up at such an opportunity claiming to be too 'punk' or 'real' but to me it was the perfect chance to get ourselves out there. We had the right attitude along the lines of, we're a band, we've got an album, look at us, listen, and you just might learn something along the way.

Mad Mike informed me that Maia Celeste had just secured the cover of Rolling Stone magazine for a band with no album but I had no regrets about flipping a coin and appointing Ted.

To tell you the truth I was relieved to be free of the mental shackles that had held me back for so many years. Years of planning operations to the last detail, worrying about what could go wrong. Years of inventive and creative sex with my wife, trying to have the perfect marriage.

As Clint Eastwood said, "We've come this far, let's not ruin it by thinking.'

Well I was no longer thinking. And it felt great.

Death By Milkshake

I never knew what it meant to be,
A guy with a friend who could eat so much cheese,
But now it's just me and I'm starting to think,
That this whole friendship thing can end in a blink,
Cause people seem to die and I never know why,
God makes up his mind and leaves me to cry

(chorus)

Death by milkshake,
It's no way to go,
But I know you're still somewhere,
Even though it's not here,
I miss you my friend, and your memories are dear

Sometimes I feel like I'm a complete fake,
Then I think of you and your favourite steak,
Mushrooms, cheese and some pepper to go,
It's really too bad that I'm here all alone,
I don't want to shed any more tears,
So I sit with a scowl and I drift through the years

(chorus)

Death by milkshake,
It's no way to go,
But I know you're still somewhere,
Even though it's not here,
I miss you my friend, and your memories are dear

So think of me Jimmy, wherever you are,
I know you'll be happy and you won't go far,
I still believe that we'll meet someday,
And God only knows that I'm staying sp brave,
The days of school seem so far away,
So I'm writing this song to remember those days

(chorus)

Death by milkshake,
It's no way to go,
But I know you're still somewhere,
Even though it's not here,
I miss you my friend, and your memories are dear

Our First Tour

Following the release of, 'You Can Keep Your Hair For All I Care" we piled into the back of a luxury stretch bus that I paid for with Nathan Nerdanté's money from a dead relative.
We weren't big enough in the states but the album had gone down pretty well in Europe so we managed book ourselves on the 'Mentalist Bender' tour supporting 'The Sand Dunes' (Beach Boy cover band) and Swedish techno duo 'Sexy Dull', who had just gone platinum with their latest album. It was a pretty strange mix but our think our different styles complemented each other well.

The tour bus was sweet and as a thank you I made sure Nathan came along for the ride but I didn't give him a bed as I felt if we were the guys playing every night we'd need our sleep.

As a band we didn't seem to spend as much time together as I thought we would. I'd always grown up thinking that touring was the time when the magic happened, when friendships deepened, and you learnt more about each other than your own family. It didn't really work that way with us.

Super Rob spent a lot of his time cycling off with the sound crew at each venue, trading advice on making kebabs He was putting on more and more weight too which I thought was having a negative impact on his guitar playing.

Wherever we went, everyone wanted to talk to Super Rob about something, and he just rode that damn bike of his (very slowly) around each venue going from one group to another.

Mad Mike was going overload with his fitness schedule and constantly stressing out that there was nowhere to surf. It got so bad that he started using our equipment to make his own gym, doing weights with the speakers and chin ups on our bunk beds in the bus. I was pretty sure he was taking amphetamines too but I didn't have time to investigate properly.

Cup Man was just hitting on every single girl that came within fifty yards of us, but when it came to show time he gave it everything he had so I couldn't really have any complaints.

I understand what it's like to be that into women and all I can say is that I'm just grateful I've never really had to work hard to get them. Women tend to gravitate towards me in a way I've never been able to explain but Cup Man is someone who enjoys the chase, or the game, whatever you want to call it.

I had my own problems to deal with the first being that I was sure The Sand Dunes had been talking shit about us behind our backs.

When we hit Milan I waited for them to go onstage before sneaking in to their dressing room disguised as a sandwich boy. I had plenty of sandwiches on my tray but hiding amongst them was my preferred spy kit consisting of the usual:

GSM Bugs
Bionic Ear
Button size cameras

USB keylogger (in case we were getting dissed on the intenet)

Whilst everyone else hit the streets of Milan to party the night away I stayed on the bus and went through my data. I drew a blank.

David the lead singer had made one call to his Mother back in California. Bobby, the bass player had spent about twenty minutes talking with Richie the drummer about whether people who believed in Scientology were total fucking idiots or just unfortunate souls who were lost.

The guitarist (whose name I forgot) made a phone call to some guy in England, then surfed the internet looking at cut price refrigerators.

What made it even more annoying was that they all seemed like nice guys, in fact, I felt I should have been out with them and the others instead of stalking them like a weirdo.

I kept this ritual up after every show, and it started to put a visible distance between my band mates and I

I couldn't tell them what I was really doing, they wouldn't understand. I was also growing a little suspicious of our tour manager, Louis.

Louis Grease was a fifty something man who'd made a name for himself booking out arenas for bands like the Chili Peppers back in the day when the scene was peaking in Hollywood.

The guy knew pretty much everyone that mattered in our business and it didn't take long for me to spend the rest of Nathan's trust money to book him as our own tour manager.

But even after all his hard work I couldn't help but notice Louis' diet on tour. It seemed like every day he ordered exactly the same three meals:

Breakfast- *A bowl of Cheerios, one banana, one cup of black coffee and orange juice*
Lunch- *Pork chops, brown rice and steamed broccoli*
Dinner- *Lamb Chops, new potatoes and peas*

Chops. Why did it have to be Chops all the time? The answer was obvious. He worked for Zack Mackchops.

All I had to do was prove it, without interrupting the tour.

I had been lucky that music had saved me when it did. Zack Mackchops and all the other hair related bullshit was supposed to be in the past.

Sometimes the past has a funny way of catching up to you.

The paranoia slowly built up as we powered our way through Europe. I hired my own camper van to drive around in and give me some much needed privacy. I didn't know who to trust anymore and for all I knew my own band mates had joined forces with The Sand Dunes.

I was still spying on them every day but had found no evidence to back up my feelings They may have been so well trained that the backstabbing was saved for onstage when they could make hand signals to each other or whisper covertly amongst the thousands of screaming fans.

I finally cracked after our Paris show. We'd performed a mediocre set and the crowd had thrown dead snails at us. One even went in my mouth and I bit down on it, getting a real shock as the crunchy shell mixed with the cold and gooey torso. It tasted like cold algae.

Backstage everyone was carrying on like it was the best show ever, drinking beers, playing games and generally having a great time. It was as though that was the idea of touring the world with your best friends playing music to thousands of adoring people. I didn't really get it myself.

"Jesus Trey, lighten up will ya? This is party time!"

I looked up to find Louis standing in front of me holding a fresh beer, dangling it like bait.

"Yeah, you'd like that wouldn't you Louis. You'd love me to take that beer and slowly get drunk. Well let me tell you something dickhead. I'm on to you."

Louis looked taken aback.

"Trey what are you talking about?"

That's when I heard the singing.

Happy birthday to you,
Happy Birthday to you,
Happy Birthday dear Trey,
Happy Birthday to you

There were flashing lights as cameras popped. Behind me a huge crowd had formed. I could make out my band mates and some of the usual tech crew but the others could have been anyone. I turned back to Louis who was smiling once again.

"Come on Trey, you didn't think you could keep your birthday a secret did you?"

Everyone was silent now and all eyes were on me. Was it really my birthday? What day was it? Where the hell was I?

Maybe Zack Mackchops had hired everyone in the room. This was a sick game. I had to think fast.

"Ready to make a wish Trey?"

Super Rob was standing there holding my cake, candles lit. I lunged forward and grabbed it from him.

"Everybody stay back! Just stay back or I swear to God I will drop this cake on the floor!"

The crowd stepped back a little, but Super Rob came a little closer.

"Trey, come on man, we spent a lot of time making that cake for you. What's wrong?"

I nodded my head in the direction of Louis.

"You can't trust that guy Super Rob. You don't know who he is."

Super Rob look puzzled.

"What the hell are you talking about?"

No! Please not Super Rob. I couldn't bear to think that they'd gotten to him too.

I could see The Sand Dunes whispering to each other in the corner. One of them laughed. It was about all I could take.

"Hey, you know what? You guys don't even sound anything like The Beach Boys!"

And with that I threw the cake high in the air and ran for the exit door in the corner of the room.

I heard the cries as the beautiful Vanilla and Chocolate masterpiece splattered on the floor but I was already out into the fresh Parisian night.

The air was cool and reviving, I started to think straight again.

All this touring, the rock n' roll lifestyle. Too many late nights and too much Starbucks. Way too much Starbucks, in fact, I ccouldn't even remember going to Starbucks as someone was always sent for me.

Louis had me so loaded up with sugar, caffeine and syrup that I'd practically lost my mind. There was someone I had to call.

"Hello?"

"Jess? Sweetheart?"

"Trey? Is that you?"

Jessica. The love of my life. I'd been so selfish. So focused on become the biggest selling artist of all time. And for what?

"Jess. Jessica, are you okay?"

It was so good to hear her voice.

"Trey where are you?"

"I'm coming home babe. That's all the matters now. I'm so sorry for leaving you."

The line went dead. Dammit. Out of money. I could hear police sirens in the distance. They must have been alerted to the cake incident. I didn't know whether it was an offence to destroy a beautiful dessert in France but I sure didn't want to find out.

I pulled my hoodie up firmly over my bald head and ran through the darkness towards the airport.

Back To Reality

The past few years had been crazy to say the least. A lot's happened that's impacted my life in various ways, good and bad, but if I had to do it all again I wouldn't hesitate.

So much of my life went into fighting hair related crimes all over the world that to deny it would be unhealthy. Although I'm keen to stress that I am against violence in general, I can never rule out the fact that it's a reality in our everyday lives.

Once you've gone as deep as I have you can never really just walk away, but I'd like to think that I can separate myself from that world, even if it's just for short moments.

I will continue with the music, and I've just started to talk again with the other guys from Bald 172. A lot of stuff was said that we can't take back, and I've accepted full responsibility for my irrational and often bizarre behaviour.

I can't see another album coming anytime soon, but none of us are calling it quits just yet. I'm hoping to meet up with the guys soon and in the meantime I've wished them all the best with their other side projects.

Right now I'm just enjoying being back home with my wife and son. Jessica has been a complete and utter rock to me and I just feel so lucky to have her in my life.

Little Trey has just started to talk which is just amazing, and I'm learning how to be a better father all the time.

I haven't seen or heard from Zack Mackchops for some time now. If he ever wants to enter my life again, I'll be ready. In the meantime, I can only pray for him.

Three Months Later

Things are really quiet round here. I haven't really been in touch with anyone outside of my family since I got back, and I've managed to nail down a pretty regular routine at home.

8.00- Wake up. Help Jess get ready for work.
8.15- Give Trey Jr his breakfast and put him in the car for school
8.18- Wave goodbye as Jess drives Trey Jr to school before going to work
8.20- Make a cup of tea
8.25- Hang upside down in the garage to encourage blood flow to the scalp
8.30- Watch an episode of Las Vegas
9.00- Watch another episode of Las Vegas
9.30- Make some tea
9.32- Watch an episode of Two and a Half Men
10.00- Check the E! channel for any Hollywood news in case I'm on it
10.15- Download some episodes of Brothers and Sisters
10.20- Watch my West Wing box set with some coffee
11.30- Go to town to buy a magazine and have a coffee
13.00- Return home and fill out one or two online job applications
14.00- Spend a few hours in my home studio working on some new music
16.00- Greet Jess and Trey Jr and ask them how their day was
16.15- Take Trey Jr to a friends house so I can spend some time with Jess alone
18.00- Jess goes to collect Trey Jr. I watch The Simpsons
19.00- Jess makes supper and puts Trey Jr to bed

20.00- Jess and Trey time

It's been a really good period for me and all in all I think it's exactly what I've needed to get my head back together, but I've started to realise that life is short and I've fallen into a comfort zone. At my age I should still be out there, competing at the top level no matter what it is I choose to do.

I didn't want to upset Jess with my thoughts so one night I spoke to a friend of mine in the local pub.

He suggested I set up a Facebook account to boost my social life. I'd never considered myself as unpopular but when I looked back on the previous few months I hadn't exactly been the man about town either.

Trey Bald Joins Facebook

I waved goodbye to my wife and kid and hurried back inside. In the kitchen I had the laptop out and ready to go, with the kettle already boiled. Once I had my tea I sat down to set up the account.

I was up and running in ten minutes. User friendly would have been an understatement. This site was the business.

I called my friend to tell him.

"Ricardo, It's Trey. I'm on Facebook. What do I do now?"

The next five minutes were intense. It was almost like being back in the field again. I had a lot to learn. I grabbed for a pen and some scrap paper and began to scribble down everything Ricardo told me.

Adding friends

Status update
Tagging photos
Adding photos
Applications
Groups
Profile Picture
Facebook chat
Relationship status
Events
Personal information

It seemed like a lot to take in and I felt overwhelmed. I hadn't even checked to see if bald/balding people where allowed to use the site.

"Of course they are stupid! Are you insane?"

Ricardo put my mind at ease. He seemed like a level headed guy. Maybe I was being a little too serious. I could see why this was such a popular site.

Trey Bald Has Problems With Facebook

Saturday morning. Trey Jr was crying about something, but I didn't know what. Jess was kicking up a fuss in the living room, I could hear doors slamming. My attention was focused on the photo on the screen.

Ricardo had tagged a photo of me.

Every time I moved the damn mouse arrow over my head my name kept appearing on the screen. The photo showed Ricardo, his wife, and I, enjoying a barbeque in someone's garden. Sitting right in between the happy couple, who both sported lovely hair, I looked like a bald peasant.

There was a little alcohol induced redness under each eye, and my skin was much paler in comparison to theirs. If this was some kind of joke I wasn't laughing. The words kept running through my head.

Ricardo Schwartz tagged a photo of you.

That was the e mail alert I found waiting for me. Initially I was excited but the reality was dire. Was this what Facebook was about?

I hear Jess call me. She sounded upset. Trey Jr was still crying.

"In a minute babe!"

I had to figure this whole thing out. God knows how many people across the world would have access to this photo.

I slipped out the back door and sneaked through the back door of Ricardo's house. I'd gotten to know him in the local pub. We would talk about sports and our wives, and with him only living three doors down it made him my only true friend.

Friendship counted for nothing at this point. He looked startled to see me as I crept through his conservatory and into the kitchen.

"Trey? Good morning to you Sir."

I motioned for his wife and daughter to leave the room.

"Could you give us a minute please?"

They left the room looking as puzzled as Ricardo.

“Is it a good morning Ricardo?”

I pulled out the baseball bat concealed under my jacket.

Ricardo’s eyes widened in shock. I got straight to the point.

“I’m going to be staright with you Ricardo. You’re a smart man. How the hell did you make a bad picture of me appear on the internet and why is my name attached to it?”

“What?”

I smashed the bat down on his daughter’s goldfish bowl. I heard his wife scream out from the next room. Ricardo called out to her.

“Tiffany it’s fine just stay out there!”

He got the point.

“Okay, just calm down Trey. That’s a photo from Steven’s barbeque a few weeks ago remember? All I did was upload it and tag you.”

“Slow down! You think I’m some kind of tech whizz? Just tell me how I get rid of it!”

Ricardo scribbled on a bit of paper.

“Just follow these instructions. Simply click on remove tag with the left hand button on your mouse.”

I snatched the paper and put it in my pocket. Then I swiftly filled a glass of water and dropped the goldfish in just in time. I wasn't some kind of animal, but I needed that information.

"I'll be seeing you around Ricardo."

And with that I left as quick as I'd arrived. I had to get rid of this photo.

The Friend Request

I awoke at three a.m. Jess was sound asleep, purring like a cat. I could hear the rain battering the windows above me.

Creeping downstairs I found the safe and familiar glow of my laptop screen. There had been some activity. I had a friend request!

Marie Olivier has added you as a friend.

It couldn't be.

Marie from Biarritz. How had she found me? When I wrote about the girl from Biarritz I thought that would be the last time I thought of her. Just what kind of a curve ball was fate throwing me now?

I quickly accepted her friend request and examined her profile. She was as beautiful as the day I'd last seen her. I was thankful to be rid of my bald photo before she came back into my life.

Jumping from one photo to the next I remembered exactly why I'd stalked her and risked my own life and reputation.

Marie was beauty defined. Here eyes pulled you in like the first display of Easter Eggs every year in the high street. Her lips were so sexual they could have been classified as a military weapon.

And her hair flowed so thick and freely, it was almost as if hair had been taken away from every bald man just for her. I reached out and tried to touch her. But it was no use.

Then I saw something else jumping from the screen. It was unexpected and it made my stomach flip repeatedly. The rain sounded like it was getting harder now and I felt the security of my house slip away. It was like staring up the barrel of a gun and wondering if you were going to be picking up pieces of your head in the following seconds.

Relationship Status:
In a relationship with
Franc Lizou

It was almost as if she'd added me as a friend to show how happy she was without me.

I needed to retaliate and quickly. Damage limitation was the order of the day. I promptly typed in a status update.

Remembering what Ricardo had taught me about Facebook etiquette, or 'netiquette' I chose my words very carefully.

Trey Bald is feeling really really good. Life is sweet.

The ball was back in her court now. I made myself a peppermint tea and crept back upstairs. It's funny how you can get out of bed and return with your life completely turned upside down.

I lay down and turned so that I could watch Jess sleeping.

Poor thing. She didn't deserve to be caught up in this mess.

Four hours later I hurried downstairs to check Marie's profile. She'd been tagged in a photo. Her name appeared when I ran the mouse arrow over those beautiful eyes.

It appeared that the man with her was her boyfriend Franc. His name also appeared when I ran the arrow over it. He was good looking and they looked like they were having lots of fun.

Touché Marie. Touché indeed. But my problems went a lot further than her new photo.

I had two new wall posts. The first one was from Mad Mike, and it was innocent enough.

Hey Trey, long time brother, hope things are all good. Drop me a line soon.

I liked Mike. He never dwelt on things, just got on with it. But I didn't have time for that just yet. I was staring in disbelief at the second wall post which was from an old school acquaintance by the name of Dan Carter.

Trey! You finally made it on to Facebook! Where you been all this time? Where's the hair gone?

Fucking Dan Carter.

I never really liked him at school and now he does this? I thought the one picture I had up was taken in a dark enough room to give off the impression of a tidy and short crew cut, a bit like a Marine.

If Marie had seen that wall post then she'd think the following four things about me.

1. I was the object of fun.
2. The butt of jokes.
3. Loser.
4. Someone who just wasn't accustomed to winning things.

This time I didn't need Ricardo's help. I managed to locate the 'delete' option myself.

Back To Biarritz

I told Jess I had an emergency meeting with the band to discuss a new album. She didn't seem convinced but then she and I had barely spoken since I'd signed up to Facebook.

I told myself it wasn't her fault if she didn't want to move with the times, but in reality I pitied her normal conversations and afternoon tea with real people.

Facebook had enabled me to create a virtual world and although things had been going wrong I had begun spending an extra four hours a day online in order to build up the perfect personality and image I'd always dreamed of having.

In the meantime I was cruising through Gatwick airport all ready to jump on the flight to Biarritz so I could put this Marie situation to bed once and for all.

I arrived at check in and handed my passport over. The man at the desk asked me to wait a moment and then whispered something into his phone. I had no cause for concern, especially with the heightened level of security in airports these days. I was already thinking about what I'd say to Marie when I found her.

"Excuse me Mr. Bald could you come with me please?"

Standing next to me was a man in a security uniform.

"What's the problem?"

He didn't flinch.

"If you could just come with me sir."

I was taken into one of those side doors that you assume is a cupboard for cleaning supplies but there was a desk and two chairs as well as one of the nicest looking coffee machines I'd seen.

The security guard had read my mind.

"Please help yourself to a cappuccino. It's free."

He turned and left the room, locking the door behind him. What the hell was going on?

I sat down and sipped on my cappuccino. It tasted great. Really great. So great, that for a moment I couldn't care less about what trouble I was or wasn't in.

Moments later, two men in suits entered the room. One was massive the other was fairly normal. They both had nice hair, but not so much so that you wanted to touch it.

The massive man spoke first.

"Mr. Bald do you know why you're here?"

"No."

They both looked at each other, then back at me. It was the turn of the normal guy to speak.

"Trey. Can I call you that?"

"Sure."

"Well, Trey. We have a situation. Earlier today we received some pretty solid intelligence that a bald man was planning an attack on the airport. We're unsure of the nature of the attack but we believe it may be chemical and potentially threatening to many thousands of people."

Typical. Just when I thought I'd escaped prejudice for at least one day.

"I'm not bald."

The massive man fired back.

"Excuse me?"

"I said, I'm not bald. I just have very thin hair. If you look closely, you'll see that aside from the obvious show of flesh in the crown area I have a fairly respectable amount of hair."

The massive guy was unconvinced.

"Mr. Bald please. Just let go. You are classified as bald."

The normal guy chimed in to make me feel a little better.

"Balding. You could be described as being in the process of balding."

I could take that.

"Maybe, yes. Well, yes, I'm balding. But I'm not bald. And you say the suspect was described as bald."

The two men looked at each other. They knew I had them. They had nothing on me.

"Mr. Bald we will allow you to leave but we will need to check your luggage and give you a full search. That includes a cavity search."

"Fine," I snapped.

It didn't matter. I was travelling light for this little trip. They'd find nothing.

Despite the inconvenience I was able to find an internet café and squeeze in a quick thirty minutes of Facebook.

I added new friends and checked my wall. There had been no recent activity. I overheard two girls talking about Facebook. One was teaching the other how to use it. I strained my neck to hear more.

"So, these are applications, and the more you have on your page the more popular you'll look 'cos it will look like people sent them to you."

I had no idea what they were talking about. Probably nothing too important, Ricardo would have told me if it was.

I was a little worried about the number of friends I had. Most people seemed to have five hundred or more and I was yet to hit two hundred.

I used the find friends through e mail tool and added every single hit that came up. I felt that would help to up the numbers so I signed off to reward myself with an Aero from the shop.

On the plane I closed my eyes and tried to relax.

Temptation At The Airport

It should have been so easy. Collect my bags, breeze through passport control and catch a cab into the town. Life can be a funny thing though, and as I moved towards the exit I felt a twitch in my left arm.

Was it a twitch or an urge? Whatever it was, it was slowly taking control of my body. I had to check my Facebook profile.

My hands were shaking now as I turned the corner ignoring the duty free shops and annoying children running around with their brand new airport toys.

It seemed like forever but I managed to locate a small collection of computers in the south west corner of the airport. Within minutes I was logged on to my account.

I had more friends, a lot more friends. Some of the people were individuals I'd only known through a few e mails, and now they were my friends! This was the kind of life I could get used to. I had more friends than I could count and I didn't make any effort, I just clicked a mouse!

I decided to experiment with the Facebook chat gizmo in the bottom right hand corner of the screen. I started typing instant messages to a friend of mine called Tom. Tom had just broken up with his girlfriend of two years and she'd deleted him as a friend.

What made things worse, was that Tom had asked a mutual friend to go to his ex-girlfriends profile page and see what she'd been doing. His ex-girlfriend had put up a new profile picture that showed her with another man. It looked like they were having a lot of fun.

I sympathised with Tom as I knew exactly how he felt. If only he knew that was the very reason I'd flown to France.

I left the chat and focused on my personal information. Maybe I hadn't made it clear enough what kind of a person I was. I decided to edit the information on my page. I added 'Weekend at Bernies' to my favourite films and 'Bondi Rescue' to my favourite tv shows.

Bondi Rescue was a great little reality show that followed the lifeguards on Bondi Beach in Sydney, Australia. I'd met them during the whole escapade at The Ivy nightclub and asked if I could be on the show to which the answer was no. I'm fairly sure it was because of my thin hair, but I never argue with a natural life saver. If that was the way it had to be then that was the way it had to be.

Next up, I decided to add some of my favourite quotes. This was tough. I wanted to pick a selection of quotes that made me seem funny, intelligent and laid back in equal measure. I couldn't afford to get this wrong.

"Excuse me, are you Trey Bald?"

I looked up to see a beautiful blonde haired girl. Before I responded I felt a sharp pang my neck and everything went black.

Catching Up With An Old Friend

My vision cleared and I found myself in a light room. That was strange, normally when I found myself knocked out for kidnapping my eyes opened to a dark room. This room was surprisingly normal.

"You know something Trey? If you wanted to remain anonymous, you really should have opened up a Myspace account instead of a Facebook one."

Zack Mackchops. He'd found me, and I didn't even see him coming.

"Mackchops. What the hell do you want from me?"

I could see him now. He was sitting at an impressive looking Apple computer on the left hand side of the room.

"You see Facebook is a fairly personal site. Although you can create a false image to some degree, the site relies on its integrity. In other words, you won't last for very long trying to be someone your not."

"But everyone does it on Facebook," I replied.

"Yes they do, but the point is people *know* that. In reality, you're not fooling anyone. That hot girl from school knows you're stalking her and that guy knows you're not really a high flying insurance broker. Don't you see Trey? Facebook is far too incestuous."

"So what makes Myspace so special?"

I was feeling awake now, but the throbbing pain in my neck reminded me I was still in a dangerous situation.

"I'm glad you ask. MySpace is the ultimate home ground for any dreamer. It doesn't focus on what school you went to, or what friends you have in common with anyone else. Instead you are free to just add people as your friend at random, and even decorate your page in different colours and strange flashing banners."

That sounded stupid, I thought to myself.

"That sounds stupid."

Mackchops looked amused at this.

"In some ways yes. But it's actually very clever. Did you know Myspace makes far more money than Facebook? In fact, using their free for all methodology, users have managed to create a world so devoid of reality, that they have even diagnosed over one million cases of MySpace Schizophrenia in America alone."

I thought about this for a moment.

"So what your saying is that Myspace is destroying social interaction and concentration spans?"

"Exactly," beamed Mackchops. "And it's only going to get worse. People who fail to make real friends will simply find them online, yet never truly know them as people. Long and pleasant dinner parties will be replaced by vicious online debates about the most pointless of topics and before you know it, they will all eventually kill each other."

My god. He was right.

"I've seen this before. Like the comments people make under YouTube videos. They all seem to be spiteful and argumentative. If nothing's done, the anger will slowly build and we'll be looking at a war on a scale like we've never seen before."

Zack clapped his hands slowly and mockingly.

"And all this time you thought the worlds troubles were a result of thick hair or hair loss."

I'd been so stupid. Maybe Zack Mackchops was right. But it didn't change the fact that he'd killed Jimmy.

"So what do we do now," I asked.

"I know why you're here in Biarritz, Trey. It's pathetic. So I'm here to help you, but I don't think you'll see it that way."

"Help me? What about killing my best friend?"

He sighed as if this question was getting tired.

"Don't you get it yet? Jimmy *had* to go, there was no other option. If fat people start believing that they deserve acceptance and credibility, what do you think would happen to normal people? We'd be over powered. Normal and slim people are the ones that get up and work hard to keep the world in order. Fat people are always lazy and there are far more of them than normal people. If we give them self confidence they would only over power us and make a mess of the perfect world we created!"

He was right.

"You and I will never see eye to eye Trey. But frankly, with your poor excuse for hair it's not something I'll lose sleep over. I hope you enjoy your new Facebook profile, but don't expect Marie to be lusting over you."

And with that, he got up and left the room. Dammit, I had to get to that computer and quickly. I struggled against the rope that held me to the chair but it was no good.

I gave up struggling and tried to sum up just what the hell I was doing tied to a chair somewhere in Biarritz. I'd left my family at home over a relationship status concerning a girl who probably never liked me in the first place. I'd experienced feelings of insecurity so strong that I'd actually jumped on a plane, all from a photo of the same girl with another man.

What the hell was happening? I could remember life before the internet, when Jess and I would stay inside on the weekends, drinking tea and playing Scrabble or watching old French films late at night whilst we planned our future together.

Life wasn't like that anymore. It was all about instant gratification and using Facebook to stalk girls that you desperately wanted to sleep with. Where had it all gone wrong?

To top it all off, I was still balding and it didn't look like stopping anytime soon. I didn't even know what side I was fighting for anymore. Was I pro bald or anti? Maybe if I had luscious hair I would have slept with the girl from Biarritz years ago and would have never been sitting here right now.

I felt the hairnergy rise inside me, like a waking beast. I broke through the rope like it was a daisy chain and sprung from the chair as if I'd been jabbed with a cattle prod. The shock of the adrenalin nearly made me faint, I hadn't planned on using my hairnergy but then I was still learning how to control it even after so many years.

Looking at the computer screen I saw the first bit of damage. My new status update read:

Trey Bald is very, very, very bald. He is losing his hair and fast…form an orderly queue ladies!

I cleared my status and read on further. Oh no. Photos.

Whilst I had been unconscious Zack Mackchops had put me in a very bright photo studio with brilliant white walls and extremely powerful spot lights.

The effect was devastating. I looked pale to the point of a corpse, and the light penetrated through my thin hair and shone magnificently off my scalp. These were without a doubt the worst photos I had ever seen of myself.

There was more.

I was now a member of over ten bald groups and my interests were all bald related too. Under quotes, it said:

Being bald may look bad, but at least I'm alive, even though I can't get any girls.

This time he'd gone too far. I always thought about killing Zack Mackchops when he took Jimmy away from me. But now that he'd hacked into my Facebook profile and done this, I was never so sure about anything in all my life. He had to go.

Something made me hesitate. It was the words that he'd spoken before leaving. They seemed to resonate in my head.

If fat people start believing that they deserve acceptance and credibility, what do you think would happen to normal people? We'd be over powered. Normal and slim people are the ones that get up and work hard to keep the world in order. Fat people are always lazy and there are far more of them than normal people. If we give them self confidence they would only over power us and make a mess of the perfect world we created!

Surely I didn't agree with that. But a part of me did. And then there were his views on the internet.

People who fail to make real friends will simply find them online, yet never truly know them as people. Long and pleasant dinner parties will be replaced by vicious online debates about the most pointless of topics and before you know it, they will all eventually kill each other.

I needed to get home and figure this out. I had no desire to track down Marie. All I wanted was to be at home with my family. I was beginning to have conflicting emotions over Zack Mackchops.

Was he an evil genius or did he really see the world clearer than anyone else?

Back Home In The Safety Zone

"How was your meeting," asked Jess, interrupting my episode of Las Vegas.

"It was great babe. Can I get a coffee?"

Jess left the room and got busy with our fancy Italian machine. I had things to figure out, just as soon as I finished Las Vegas.

Since my trip I knew I'd have to put some time into researching fat people and social networking on the internet. I too had once been a little on the fat side, and I struggled to remember whether I had a negative impact on my surroundings.

As for social networking on the internet, I was still fairly new to it, but I knew that since I'd joined Facebook I'd ignored my wife and son and flown to France to chase a girl who had a boyfriend and didn't like me.

But she did add me as a friend, so there may have been some lingering feelings there.

I was so confused. There was only one person I could call now.

Johnny Be Good

As I waited for an answer I felt a few nerves. This was a tricky phone call to make.

"Yeah?"

"Captain Dynamite, good morning sir."

"Trey is that you? You sound upset. I'll be there in ten."

The line went dead. I relaxed.

Exactly ten minutes later there was a loud rap on the door. Without waiting for an answer Johnny Dynamite strode into the room, taking it over as usual. Jess appeared in the doorway and immediately blushed.

I'd never felt bad about her obvious attraction to the great man. To be bitter about it would be a waste of time and would only force her into his arms. If I was going to be a man I would have to trust her.

"Trey, I got here as soon as I could."

His eyes glanced over to Jess.

"Jessica. You look sexy as hell, no surprise there."

Jessica giggled and looked away. I took affirmative action.

"Honey, why don't you take Trey Jr out to the park for ten minutes?"

Alone with Captain Dynamite, I pressed for answers. I told him everything that had happened, and how I was failing to be a good father and husband.

"You worry too much Trey. I'll give it to you straight. Social networking is for lonely people. Maybe once in a while it can be fun if you don't take it seriously, but otherwise don't bother. You need to get up earlier, swim fifty lengths or go for a run, then eat a big breakfast. Trust me, you'll get ten times as much done during the day with that routine."

I thought about it and I knew he was making sense. Captain Dynamite continued.

"Here's what I'm going to do for you. I will help you financially if you ever need it, but you have to either get your band producing the goods or hold down a steady job. No more craziness, no more random trips away from home. You need to save your marriage. I could have taken Jess there and then on the living room floor. It would have been sensational, especially for her."

He was right. I started to take notes.

"Look at me Trey. I'm good looking, fit and healthy and I control the entire world. How do I do it? With discipline and a solid daily routine. I don't go around following whatever new idea enters my head. I take care of what needs to be done. Now it's time for you to find something new in your life. You've had a lot of luck so far, long may it continue."

"What about my hair," I asked.

"Come on Trey. You can't have everything. You know how bad I feel for you and your male pattern baldness, but there's nothing we or anyone else can do about it. Yet. Now let's go and join your beautiful wife and son in the park."

And just like that I felt like a new man.

As I walked to the park with Captain Dynamite's arm around my shoulders, I began to feel as though I'd been given a second chance in life. No one could ever know why Captain Dynamite was always on hand to help me but I also liked to think I could call him a friend too.

But I still had a lot of enemies out there.

"I want you, Jessica and Trey Jr to come and hang out with me in my holiday house."

I looked up at Captain Dynamite. It felt weird, only seconds earlier in my head I had been creating the end of a long chapter in my life and now it seemed as though things were going to continue at the same hectic pace.

Johnny Dynamite's holiday house? How good would that be? What if he stole my wife and kid?

"Sounds good to me Captain," I replied.

Flying First Class

Captain Dynamite's private jet is something you have to see to believe. The seats are made from leather that seems to suck your body into them whilst simultaneously giving you a massage until your deepest concerns have left you, leaving you with a feeling that's nothing short of euphoric.

But I'm old enough to know that everything costs something. I didn't want to skip around the subject anymore and once Jess and Trey Jr were sleeping soundly at the back I took up a seat right across from Captain Dynamite who was nursing a gin and tonic and speaking on the phone.

His tie was loosened now and he appeared relaxed, but my presence caused him to cut short the phone call and lean forward. A classic people person, he made you feel like you were the only living being in the world.

"You didn't invite me to your house for a simple holiday did you Captain?"

Captain Dynamite let out a half smile, like a ten year old boy who knows he's been naughty. He sank back into his chair and looked away, stirring his drink.

"You're right Trey, I didn't invite you for just a holiday," he replied, still looking away from me.

"Captain Dynamite, you know you don't have to ask me twice. Just tell me what needs to be done Sir."

He looked straight at me, and the cheeky smile had been replaced with a look that means business.

"You're the only person I can trust Trey. I'm only sorry to drag your family into the matter. If it's any consolation, I really do expect them to holiday at my house."

"I get the impression you and I won't be joining them."

A delightful looking air hostess appeared to tell us to prepare for landing. Captain Dynamite thanked her politely and turned back to me.

"Let's enjoy the next few days Trey. Our business can wait, I promise. I want you to have a little fun."

And with that he gave me the winning smile that made you want to simultaneously climb the highest mountain and graduate from a top Law school. I was in. No doubt about it.

The jet began its descent and I watched the clouds give way to a beautiful landscape of blue water and golden sands. The long journey that I thought was over seemed to be just beginning.

And I hadn't even thought about checking my Facebook profile.

The Calm Before The Storm

You'll forgive me for not revealing the exact location of Captain Dynamite's home. All I can say is that the following two or three days were some of the best in my life. By day I enjoyed the private beach with my family.

It was an amazing feeling to run my son towards the incoming waves and retreat at the last minute, hearing his laughter ring through my ears and seeing my beautiful wife watching us from her spot on the warm sand.

Occasionally Captain Dynamite would join us for a swim as he kept his finely tuned body in peak condition, but he never interfered in the private time Jess and I had been waiting for.

On the contrary, he spent most afternoons teaching Trey Jr how to fish using his seven hundred foot yacht which they would take out to sea and anchor up.

Trey Jr could have no better role model in life. Rather than feel jealous I felt privileged to share my son with the Captain, who for reasons unknown to me, had never found time for fatherhood.

In the evening Jess and I would take a case of ice cold beers down on to the beach and play N.E.R.D (Fly or Die album) on the i-pod with the portable speakers. It was the perfect soundtrack to our new found dream like existence. I didn't want it to end. I knew the time was coming but I clung on to every last second like they were the last I had on earth.

On the third night I walked with Jess to the highest cliff top the overlooked the sprawling ocean, now covered in a blanket of shadows, hiding some of life's most beautiful and dangerous creatures.

The sound of the waves crashing against the rocks made me think of Jack Bauer at the end of 24 season six when you're wondering whether he's going to jump off the edge.

I turned to Jess in the darkness. I could smell her hair that had been washed with Herbal Essences. It was exquisite. Right then I knew it was time to say the words I'd been waiting to say for far too long.

"Jess, you're the coolest girl ever. And I love you, and after all this time, I still fancy you like you were some beautiful stranger on the bus."

We kissed each other for an eternity and we became one. In that moment, something shifted in the Universe and I knew that someone was watching over us.

The next morning I joined Captain Dynamite for coffee on the veranda. We looked out over the beach and traded old war stories, laughing at the times we'd once considered to be the most terrifying of our lives.

Jess had taken Trey Jr on an organised walk through the mountains which gave myself and Captain Dynamite a chance to get the expected game of golf out of the way. I was playing fairly below par, but he was like a man on fire. I hadn't expected anything less but I couldn't help but wonder if he'd given himself too high a handicap. He seemed as though he should have been playing off about three instead of eight.

My short game had cost me dearly and I tried to forget about it as we enjoyed the customary beer at the nineteenth hole.

"You're a little out of practice Trey," laughed the Captain.

"Maybe I should stay here a little longer till things pick up."

We laughed but it was awkward. He knew I was pressing him for the real reason I'd been invited.

"Did you ever find out why Justin Hemmings wouldn't let you in The Ivy?"

Touché Captain. Keep me distracted.

"I'm not entirely sure but I figure it's got to be something to do with my bad hair."

He thought this over as though it was an important issue.

"I'll tell you what. Why don't we work together to find out the answer, how does that sound?"

I was doubtful.

"Justin Hemmings is a successful man, he's got an army of good looking and unemployed people to defend him."

Captain Dynamite waved a hand in disgust.

"I eat good looking people for breakfast."

This was true.

With him on my side it probably wouldn't be long before I owned The Ivy. But was that what I wanted?

The time was right. I asked the question.

"What do you want from me Captain?"

His smile vanished.

"I want you to help me destroy Big Brother."

Reality TV Just Became A Lot More Real, Part I

Reality television has made a handful of people incredibly rich, there was no denying it's success. I was also aware of the controversy that surrounded it, and you couldn't flick from one comedy show to another without seeing some sort of reality television parody.

My only concern was that I couldn't see how it had anything to do with hair, and that had been my only cause for war up to this point in my life (with the exception of Jimmy's death).

Captain Dynamite had brought me into his private viewing room which housed over six hundred televisions, all broadcasting some form of reality television.

"Look at them Trey. Parading around like morons whilst they chat to each other about absolutely nothing."

He seemed angry for the first time in his life.

"With all due respect Sir, I think you just have to take shows like these with a pinch of salt."

"Don't try and sweep this crap under the carpet Trey. It represents everything that's wrong with our world today."

He was right. I knew he was right, but somehow I felt this was an issue that kept him up night upon night whilst I simply chose to ignore it. This was his war and I was the hired gun. I knew I was going to help him, my relationship with Captain Dynamite would make sure of that.

Why exactly? Because he was the man who led me to my wife.

The Advice That Changed My Life

You may recall my annual stop over in Chicago when I met an aspiring actress named Jessica. Do you remember that I said she would be my wife and she laughed right in my face? Well there's a little bit more to the story than that.

Before I was married I wasn't quite the ladies man I made myself out to be. The truth is, I struggled incredibly with my male pattern baldness and it certainly affected my confidence with women. The only thing that would pull me through would be my natural confidence that came out of the rest of my body.

Looking at the situation logically, the top of the head only covers a small percentage of the entire human body. As a result, when you have confidence leaking out of every pore, it's not going to matter much if you have a minor surface area of no confidence. It probably reduces your overall confidence by about five percent.

In my teen years I was sleeping with an average of fifteen women per week. By the time I started losing my hair, the number was more like five or seven. I tried not to let it affect me but it could be hard sometimes. And then I met a man called Johnny.

Johnny introduced himself as a software consultant but that never sat quite right with me.

I'd been speaking with him for around ten minutes when he said something unusual.

"You're a good man Trey. I can tell that about you. And behind every good man is an even better woman."

At this point I think I was more confused than anything else but there was something so damn sincere about him it was like he could just open me up and read my innermost thoughts. Coincidentally, I'd recently been thinking about how much I wanted to settle down with someone, and leave the playboy life behind me. The man named Johnny read my mind.

"There's a girl behind the bar you've been staring at this evening. I want you to go and introduce yourself."

I squirmed in my chair.

"I don't think I really feel-"

"Then tell her you're going to make her your wife. Don't let me down Trey. That right there is the finest woman in the room. One day she's going to be an excellent mother."

And just like that he got up from his chair and glided eloquently across the room, straight into a new conversation. The man had some serious class, there was no doubt about it. I had no idea I'd just met the newly appointed leader of the world.

Reality TV Just Became A Lot More Real, Part II

I sat in the back of the jeep alongside Captain Dynamite and two other men who I only knew as Bartholomew and Marcus. They would be providing tactical support from the van. Captain Dynamite seemed on edge now, as he sat there in his all black kit ready to slip into the shadows.

The plan was to infiltrate the Big Brother house (country/location not named for legal reasons) and lay down a series of timed explosives in areas intended to cause maximum devastation. The devices were nothing special, but as such short notice and with the general intellect of any Big Brother house I didn't think it would be a problem even if they did stand out a little.

Upon arrival we left Bartholomew and Marcus in the van and ran in a low crouch to the adjacent wall. Fifty metres further right was the official security gate which allowed access to members of the production team at all times.

We were over the wall in moments and Captain Dynamite immediately ripped off his black kit to reveal the standard producers outfit below. A trendy but not too extravagant jumper with a simple white shirt underneath complimented by some well cut blue jeans and half smart black loafers. To round the look off, he placed some modern square spectacles on his strong nose and looked at me.

"Let's move."

I was wearing similar attire but my shirt had a collar which I decided to wear up, and instead of black loafers I had a pair of snug white gym plimsolls which I heard that despite being the same things you wore when you were an eight year old school boy, were coming back into fashion.

We entered the production area through a side door using one of my stray hairs to delicately pick the lock.

As we made our way down the winding corridor knowing full well that the access to the official house was heavily guarded, I started to think about my family. I also couldn't understand why Captain Dynamite would expose himself like this when he had everything a man could need. I started to wonder if everyone always is as happy as they claim, and as dangerous as Captain Dynamite probably had the potential to be, violence was not really in his nature.

"Excuse me Sir, Can I see some identification?"

We were stopped by an average looking security guard. He had a skinny but fashionably dressed youth with him who must have been a runner working for free.

"Here you go my good man," replied Captain Dynamite as he smoothly revealed the world class fake identification provided by Bartholomew and Marcus. The security guard looked at the I.D. for some time before murmuring something into his radio.

"Is there a problem Sir," asked Captain Dynamite, a quizzical expression dominating his handsome face.

We were joined by another five security guards who surrounded us.

"Please put your hands on your head Sir and turn around slowly. We are going to have to call the police in."

Captain Dynamite looked shocked but did as he was told. I stood there frozen to the spot.

"But I don't understand. I'm just trying to get to work."

The security guard looked annoyed now.

"I've never seen you here before, and you're far too good looking to be working a standard production job. Everything about you screams win win and you have the audacity to strut through my building and try and con me with this impressive fake identification."

The security guard flashed a glance in my direction.

"You with this guy or what?"

"No," I replied. "Just went to the bathroom."

"Well there's nothing to see here, so you can go to work okay pal?"

I left without a fight, a million thoughts running through my head. I caught up to the fashionable youth and faked a laugh.

"I wonder why they didn't hassle me!"

The youth looked at me and then my head. I could hear his thoughts through the mass of carefully sculpted and beautifully scented hair.

Who cares what you're doing? You're bald.

What a little prick, I thought to myself as I moved on past him towards the adjoining corridor that was flocking with men and women all wearing headsets and bumping into each other like lemmings. I heard the incessant chatter of unoriginal people and began to feel sick.

Be strong Trey, you'll be out of here soon.

As I rounded the corridor I decided to make contact with Bartholomew and Marcus in the van. Pretending to cough, I uttered into my transmitter as the other members of production and catering started staring at me, clearly wondering who I was.

"Dynamite is down, do you copy?"

No response.

"Dynamite is down, do you copy?"

Something was wrong and I knew that it was only the start of my problems. By now I was gaining a lot of attention and I didn't think it would be long before the game was up. I couldn't understand why they were looking at me. I looked like part of the group, probably better looking than most but my poor hair situation allowed me to get away with that.

I was approached by a friendly looking PA who led me to one side. She almost seemed embarrassed, nothing I wasn't used to when a lady made an approach.

"I'm sorry but it's just that someone should tell you."

"Tell me what sweetheart?" I responded, keeping the pace fast and fresh.

"You're flies are undone and we can all see your willy."

Dammit. I hadn't had time to check the reliability of the jeans before we left. The mission had been far too rushed and now I was paying the price for it.

I broke away and into a sprint, looking for the nearest bathroom to hide in. It didn't take long before I found the reassuring male toilet symbol and I bundled myself into the first cubicle, locking the door and breathing heavily.

It was then that the voice sounded in my earpiece. But it wasn't Bartholomew or Marcus.

"Captain Dynamite? What's going on? You're supposed to stay off this frequency whilst we're undercover."

I could hear the regret in his voice.

"I don't have much time Trey and I'm sorry for everything. I had to save my family."

And with that, I heard the bathroom door burst open.

"FBI, freeze!"

What the hell were the feds doing here?

"I'm coming out!" I shouted, slowly unlocking my cubicle.

"Come out slowly and keep your hands where I can see them!"

The man was alone, clearly not a federal agent. He didn't even have a black jacket with FBI in yellow letters on it. Who said that watching television couldn't be useful?

I needed to find his weakness before anything else. Not knowing who or why he was here was unsettling but I had to go one step at a time.

"Okay, just relax, I'm unarmed."

I caught sight of his balding crown in the mirror behind him. Perfect. He would suffer from a slight lack of confidence for sure.

"By the way, I know how you can get thicker hair in just one week."

The temporary confusion was all I needed. Clearly not well trained he blinked for a fraction of a second as he thought about my proposal.

I lunged forward knocking the weapon from his hand before delivering a swift blow downwards into his stomach, knocking the wind from him. He fell to the ground and scrambled into the corner, desperately trying to recover his breath. I advanced on him and crouched down.

"You're going to tell me everything I need to know, it just depends on how much you want it to hurt."

The man let out a hoarse whisper.

"Zack told me you wouldn't come easily."

There was a loud explosion from somewhere further down in the corridor. I moved swiftly to the door, weapon drawn. Through the slight crack I saw people running in confusion, screams cutting through the air at a deafening level.

I turned back to my attacker.

"No!"

He was convulsing on the floor, foam appearing from the corner of his mouth.

“Spit it out, spit it out!” I shouted in vain as the cyanide tablet did its job.

“Dammit,” I muttered.

And that was when everything went silent.

No more screams, no more running. The people would be safe, I knew that. It was me they were after, and as I listened out for the neat formation of footsteps from the inevitable team assigned to capture me I sank to my knees and placed my hands behind my head. This was one situation I was going to have to ride out.

So Johnny Dynamite had a family after all. I thought about my own family once again, and the incredible time we spent on his island only days previously. I tried to block out those thoughts and stared ahead at the door.

Eventually it opened, and there was Zack Mackchops himself. A knowing look on his face that made me feel like a nuisance.

“I’m getting really tired of our meetings Trey.”

He stepped out of the way as a larger man approached me and despite seeing it coming I did nothing to stop the kick aimed right at my face.

Just like most times I came face to face with Zack Mackchops, everything went black..

EPILOGUE

To those of you who have come this far, I want to thank you for your patience. No story can be told in its entirety in such a short period of time and now that I find myself involved in a multitude of legal issues concerning the material in this book I have little idea about when I can finish what I started.

If anyone would like to donate to my legal team then please send your postal address to treybald@hotmail.com and in return I will send you a stamped addressed envelope for donations. I'll need something north of one hundred thousand pounds. If you're American, I think you just sort of half the amount and put it in dollars.

Trey